OC   '98

LOLO &
RED-LEGS

by KIRK REEVE

rising moon
Books for Young Readers from Northland Publishing

To the children of
"Las Lomitas"

The cover illustration was rendered in acrylic
and oil on Stratmore paper
The text type was set in Veljovic
The display type was set in Copacabana
Composed and manufactured in the United States of America
Designed by Billie Jo Bishop
Edited by Aimee Jackson
Spanish edited by Lou Matthews
Production supervised by Lisa Brownfield

FIRST IMPRESSION
ISBN 0-87358-683-2 (hc)
ISBN 0-87358-684-0 (sc)

Library of Congress Catalog Card Number 97-49969
Reeve, Kirk, date.
Lolo and red-legs / Kirk Reeve.

p.   cm.
Summary: When eleven-year-old Lolo captures a tarantula, it turns
an ordinary summer into a series of adventures that take him and his
friends beyond their Mexican-American neighborhood in East Los Angeles.
ISBN 0-87358-683-2. — ISBN 0-87358-684-0 (pbk.)
[1. Tarantulas—Fiction. 2. Mexican Americans—Fiction. 3. Los
Angeles (Calif.)—Fiction.] I. Title.
PZ7.R25575Lo 1998
[Fic]—dc21   97-49969

A NOTE TO THE READER

You will find Spanish used throughout *Lolo and Red-Legs*. You can usually figure out the meaning of these phrases from the English words around them. There is also a glossary with definitions and translated phrases at the end of the book (pages 110-111). *Lolo and Red-Legs* takes place in Southern California, and the Spanish in these pages reflects the language used in that region. It may be different from the Spanish you know or have heard spoken in other regions of the U. S.

1

The Best in Las Lomitas

*E*nemy scouts comin' this way!" Mario shouted. He stood close to the fort's front wall, shading his eyes with both hands as he studied the rutted asphalt of Record Avenue a stone's throw below him. The bright, summer sun was high above, and it was already hot on the hillside. "Let's get inside, Frankie!"

"You go first, man. I'm gonna be a hero and cover your big rear." Frankie fast-pitched a dirt clod into a cluster of hedgehog cactus.

"Hey, don't come in yet!" Lolo called from inside the fort. "I'm not done with the roof! It keeps fallin' down in the middle!"

"Hurry up, homes!" Frankie called back. "The war's startin'!"

"Forget the war. Gimme some more wood!"

"We only got this broomstick we were gonna use for a flagpole," answered Mario. He passed the broken handle through one of the fort's crawl-hole entrances. "You can stick it in the ground like a tent pole."

"Or stick it in your ear!" teased Frankie. "Just fix it, man, 'cause we wanna play!"

"Or stay there and hold it!" Mario added, a grin on his face.

"You're both funny as spit," grumbled Lolo. "Remind me to laugh someday."

The three dark-haired eleven-year-olds had dug their fort partway into the dry hillside halfway down from Geraghty Avenue's friendly backyards. Its front wall of boards, cement blocks, and cardboard defended against attackers coming up from Record Avenue. The cardboard roof sheltered the back half of the fort, allowing a stand-up-and-throw area just behind the front wall. The two crawl-hole entrances were on either side of the fort, strategically out-of-view behind the front wall. Inside, where Lolo struggled with the broomstick, the three had stored a pile of dirt-clod ammunition.

"That's gotta do it," said Lolo. "It's gettin' too hot in here." He lifted the front of his T-shirt to wipe beads of perspiration from his face, then stood up behind the chest-high front wall and spanked dust off his jeans. He was long-legged for his age, and slender. "How's it look?"

"Great!" said Mario, stepping back to admire their work. "It's the best fort in Las Lomitas!"

"It looks tough," agreed Frankie. Then, shaking his fist in the direction of the street below, he shouted, "And nobody better mess with it!"

Mario noticed the gesture and said, "We won't let nobody get close, Frankie. I bet we can even hit Record from here."

"One way to find out," said Lolo. "C'mon inside and let's throw some. You two need the practice anyway."

Mario squeezed his chubby body through one of the crawl-holes first. Frankie, lean but husky in his shoulders and arms, slipped through easily behind him. They picked up clods from the pile, then stood up beside the taller Lolo.

"You go first, homey," challenged Frankie. "Let's see whatcha got!"

"I don't need much to beat you!" kidded Lolo. He fingered a clod in his right hand. It felt hard and dry, and was easy to grip. He shifted his weight to his right foot, and slowly bent back with his arm cocked.

"Go for it, Lolo!" cheered Mario.

The dirt clod sailed in a high arc, easily crossed over the street, then splattered with a "thump" on the shiny hood of a '68 Chevy lowrider parked in front of one of the houses.

"Are you crazy?" Frankie shrieked as they ducked down.

"I hope not," replied Lolo, his voice shaky. "I didn't mean to hit the car!"

"Sure, Lolo," chided Frankie. "Who's gonna believe you?"

"It was an accident, Frankie! No big deal!"

"It is a big deal, homes! Those wheels belong to Rogelio's brother! That dude's mean even when he's feelin' good! We're lucky he's still in jail!"

"Geez! Rogelio's bad enough!" said Mario, swallowing hard. "I'm gonna split for home."

"Me, too," said Frankie. "How 'bout you, Lolo? This ain't no place to be right now, man."

Lolo peered over the wall to see if anyone on the street below had noticed what happened. Seeing no one, he shook his head, "I'm gonna stay for awhile and pick up some more clods. You guys sweat too much."

"Maybe you don't sweat enough," said Mario, heading for a crawl-hole. "See you later."

"Yeah, see you, Lolo," added Frankie. "Better rest your arm!"

♦ ♦ ♦

Lolo chose his dirt clods carefully. They couldn't be too small, nor could they crumble in his hand. He gathered only those that looked and felt right. He roamed about the sun-baked slope, making several trips back to the fort with all the clods he could carry. He kept an eye on Record Avenue. It remained quiet.

As he was about to quit and go home, something on the ground ahead caught his attention. Its blackness made it stand out against the reddish-brown dirt. He stepped closer—but not too close.

"Oh, man!" he said aloud. There on the sloping terrain before him was a spider—a very large spider. "Oh, man!"

It measured at least five inches wide from leg tip to leg tip, and was almost all black except for reddish-orange and tan-colored stripes around each of its eight legs. It had been motionless up until now, but as Lolo bent down to pick up a rock, it disappeared into its hole just a few inches away.

Lolo crept up to the hole, picking up a second rock on the way. He stood above it and bent down cautiously to get a closer look. He could see webbing around the opening, which narrowed to a dark circle a couple of inches in diameter.

A familiar whistle interrupted Lolo. He turned toward the houses above, set his mouth and tongue, then returned the high-pitched signal. Tossing the rocks to one side, he headed up the hill to a well-worn path that ran alongside the backyard fences and walls. When he came to his own fence, he pulled back a flap of chain link and climbed through. The coolness of his tree-shaded yard provided relief from the hot, open hillside.

"*Abuelo!*" he called to Grandfather. "I'm home."

"*Ven m'ijo.* Lunch is ready."

Lolo washed his hands in the small service porch, then sat down at the kitchen table next to Lupita, his twelve-year-old sister.

"*Abuelo!*" he said as Grandfather served him milk and a warm bean-and-cheese burrito. "I just saw a giant spider down by the fort! It's bigger than my hand!"

"Oh, yuk!" interrupted Lupita, a look of disgust on her face. "What did you do, Lolo?"

"Nothin'! It ran into a hole before I could hit it with a rock."

"I hope it stays there! It gives me shivers to think of it. A spider that big could kill you!"

"I've seen big spiders many times around Chihuahua," said Grandfather. "*Tarántulas! No son peligrosas.* They can be frightening to look at, but they don't hurt anyone. Only the insects they eat. Maybe you saw a *tarántula, m'ijo.*"

"I wish you could see it, *Abuelo.*" Lolo paused as an idea came to him. "If it is a tarantula, do you think we could catch it?"

"Don't bring any spiders up here!" warned

Lupita, her voice tense. "I'll tell Mom!"

"*Pues, vamos a ver.* We can take a look. It won't hurt," said Grandfather. He rubbed the stubble of white whiskers on his chin before continuing. *"¿Que vas a hacer con una tarántula, m'ijo?"*

Lolo thought for a moment. "I'd show it to my friends . . . maybe take it to school. I'd learn how to take care of it, *Abuelo.*"

Lupita stared unbelievingly at Lolo, then at Grandfather. "You both have to be kidding!" she yelled. "I'm gonna tell Mom!"

"*Vamos a necesitar algo para guardarla.* Look around the house, *m'ijo.* See if you can find a large can or jar."

"I'm gonna tell Mom!" insisted Lupita, her dark brown eyes wide with alarm.

"I can get an empty pickle jar from Monica's!" said Lolo, his eyes shining with excitement. "Would that be all right?"

"*Sí, m'ijo.* You get a big jar. Then we'll go look for your giant spider."

"I'M TELLING MOM!"

2

Goin' Fishin'

Isidoro "Lolo" Garcia had lived on Geraghty Avenue in *"Las Lomitas,"* the "little hills" of East Los Angeles, for all of his eleven years. He had walked up this steep, narrow street from his house to Monica's Market hundreds of times, but never with such questions on his mind as he had now. "How can we get the tarantula into a jar?" he asked himself as he reached the open entrance of the small grocery store. "How can we even get it out of its hole?"

"Hey, Lolo, my handsome young friend!" the pretty woman behind the counter greeted him. She was about his mother's age—early thirties—with shining black hair down to her shoulders and blue makeup surrounding her dark, twinkling eyes. "Are you talking to yourself? Why don't you talk to me instead? *¿En qué piensas, m'ijo?*"

"Hi, Monica. I was just thinkin' about the giant spider I saw on the hill behind my house."

"A giant spider, *m'ijo?*" Her eyes lost their twinkle.

"Yeah! It's huge, Monica! It might be a tarantula. My *abuelo* and I are gonna catch it."

"I'm scared of little spiders, *m'ijo!*" she shuddered. "Don't even talk to me about giant ones!"

"We need somethin' to put it in—like one of those great big pickle jars. Do you have an empty one we can have?"

"I probably do. I never throw 'em away. Somebody always wants one for some reason." She paused, shaking her head. "But yours . . ." She shuddered again. "*¡Ay, los muchachos!* I'll be right back."

Monica returned from the storeroom in less than a minute holding an empty gallon-size jar. "You can have this one, Lolo. It's got a lid, too."

"Thanks, Monica. I'll come back and show you the spider after we catch it!"

"No, no, *m'ijo!*" she sputtered, throwing up her hands. "I don't want to see it!"

"It's no trouble, Monica," Lolo teased as he started for the door.

"LOLO! I DON'T LIKE SPIDERS!"

◆ ◆ ◆

"Have you ever caught a tarantula before?" Lolo asked Grandfather as the two walked single file along the path to the fort.

"*No, m'ijo, pero lo ha visto como se hace.* I've seen it done. One of my *compadres* in *Chihuahua* had several *tarántulas* as pets over the years. I've seen him catch them."

"Man!" said Lolo, surprised. "I've never heard of anyone havin' a pet spider before!"

"*En México, es regular,*" said Grandfather. "Maybe here, too." He followed closely behind Lolo, sure-footed on the steep slope. He was thin-hipped and broad-shouldered like Lolo. His bushy, white mustache contrasted with his dark complexion, weathered and wrinkled from years of working outdoors. "A pet store might have information about tarantulas," he continued. "You may want to stop by the one down on Hammel Street near your school."

"There's the hole, *Abuelo!*" Lolo interrupted, pointing to the burrow. "But I don't see the spider."

"It's probably hiding just inside the hole, watching for a cricket or grasshopper to come by. Then you'd see it run out to catch its dinner. Let's see if it would like some fresh hamburger, instead."

Lolo set the jar on the ground. He watched Grandfather take a small package and some string from his shirt pocket, then unfold the paper to reveal a small amount of uncooked ground beef.

"*Necesito una piedrita como el tamaño de una moneda, m'ijo.*"

Lolo searched the ground around him. "Like this

one?" he asked, picking up a thin piece of shale about the size of a quarter.

Grandfather took the rock and placed the meat on top of it. "Now I'm going to tie one end of the string to the rock so that I can pull it. We are almost ready to lure the spider out of its burrow. Go get a piece of cardboard from your fort, *m'ijo.*"

Lolo returned with a piece he had borrowed from the front wall.

"I'm going to lower the meat in front of the burrow, *m'ijo.* When the spider grabs it, I'll pull it away from the hole. As I do, you place the cardboard between the spider and the hole so that it can't run back in. *¿Estás listo?*"

"I'm ready," replied Lolo, crouching down behind the burrow opening. He licked his lips nervously as he waited.

Grandfather slowly lowered the string until the bait rested on the ground outside the hole. Lolo hardly took a breath before the spider darted out of the hole and pounced on the meat. Grandfather pulled the rock away from the hole, taking the meat and the spider with it. Lolo forced the edge of the cardboard into the soft dirt at the entrance of the burrow, blocking any chance of retreat.

Using the jar's lid, Grandfather gently nudged the spider into the jar. "That was pretty easy!" he said.

He screwed on the lid, then handed the jar to Lolo. "*Ahora cuidala bien.* Take good care of your pet."

Lolo held the jar out in front of him, getting his first good look at the tarantula. "It's hairy, *Abuelo!* There's hair all over its body and legs!"

"*Sí, m'ijo.*"

"And its got a couple of hairy arms comin' out of its head right at me! It's scary lookin', isn't it." His voice was a little shaky. "Maybe I'd better go to the pet store right now."

"Just come home in time for dinner, *m'ijo.* Otherwise, your mom will be mad at us."

3
Animales Domésticos

The one thing Lolo liked best about living in Las Lomitas was the view from the street outside his front gate. Facing downhill, he could look at miles and miles of city spread out before him. Far off in the distance, way beyond the streets he knew, was the ocean. Sometimes he thought he could see it on clear days.

Lolo enjoyed this view now as he walked down Geraghty, his arms wrapped firmly around the pickle jar. He stayed in the middle of the street since parked cars blocked the sidewalks. A sense of freedom swept over him like the gentle breeze he was facing. Even though he had never traveled beyond the streets of East Los Angeles, this view reminded him of the many places he would like to see someday.

At the end of Geraghty, he turned left for a short block, then right onto Record Avenue. He stayed on

Record as it gradually leveled off, then turned left at Hammel Street. The pet store, "Animales Domésticos," stood by itself at the end of the block.

Lolo passed this way going to school. He had stopped at the pet store many times when Papá Rodriguez owned it. Now someone new owned the store . . . a young man Lolo had never met. The man looked up from the change he was giving a customer as Lolo entered.

"Be right with you!" the man said, his voice and smile friendly.

When the customer left, he turned to Lolo. "That's a good-looking red-leg you have there. Where did you get it?"

"I found it on the hill behind my house. My abuelo caught it for me. It's a tarantula, right?"

"Sure is! It's a Mexican red-leg. A healthy female. Set it here on the counter if you like."

"How do you know it's a female?"

"Adult males have hook-like growths under their front legs that they use during mating. This red-leg doesn't have mating hooks, so she must be a female. I had a male red-leg for a couple of years, but it died a while back."

"You had a tarantula for a pet?" Lolo asked.

"Sure! Still do. I have a Mexican brown, a Texas cinnamon, and a Honduran black velvet. I keep them at home, but pretty soon I'll set their tarantu-lariums up here in the shop. I may even get a few more and try selling them."

"What's a tar . . . tarantu . . . larium?"

"That's just a home for a pet tarantula. I prefer to use terrariums for mine. The jar you have there is your tarantularium, only you should poke a few more air holes in the lid. They need air just like you. Also, since Mexican red-legs are burrowing spiders, they should have some dirt or fine gravel to dig in, and a rock to crawl under."

"Man!" Lolo whispered, impressed by the store owner's knowledge. "What do you feed yours?"

"Most tarantulas eat big insects. I feed mine live crickets once or twice a week. I raise and sell crickets here in the shop, so *no problema*. By the way, my name's Alex Verdugo. What's yours?"

"Isidoro Garcia. Most people call me Lolo."

"I'm pleased to meet another tarantula owner, Lolo. Let's see if we can make a comfortable taran-tularium out of this jar. A beautiful red-leg like yours deserves a nice home."

Lolo took a half step backward, his eyes open-ing wide, as Mr. Verdugo removed the lid of the pickle jar, reached inside, and picked up the spider.

"Maybe I can teach you how to handle your red-leg one of these days," he said as he gently set the tarantula down in a plastic container next to the jar.

Lolo shook his head, still wide-eyed. "I'm not ready for that yet. No way!"

"You will be before long," Mr. Verdugo assured him. He poured a bag full of fish-tank gravel into the jar, then rummaged around in a box under the counter and came up with an old sponge. He cut off a small piece and took it over to a nearby sink.

"You should make sure your tarantula has water every couple of days," he advised as he lowered the wet piece of sponge into the jar. "This is a good way to do it since a spider has to crawl on top of its water source to get its mouth in position to drink. Now let's poke a few more air holes in the lid, then give your red-leg its first meal in captivity."

Mr. Verdugo returned the spider to its newly furnished tarantularium, then stepped over to a medium-size terrarium. "Here's my cricket cage," he said as Lolo joined him. Inside the terrarium, a dozen or so crickets crawled and hopped around. Mr. Verdugo picked up a short-handled fish net from the counter. He lifted the terrarium's screened roof and stuck the net down inside. One of the bigger crickets tried to hop out of the way, but got caught instead and quickly pulled out.

"Push the screen back over the cage, would you, Lolo?" Mr. Verdugo asked as he placed the net over the pickle jar's opening. With a flick of his finger, he knocked the cricket into the jar.

"Go ahead and screw the lid back on," he said. Lolo turned the lid, watching for the tarantula's reaction to the cricket. The spider remained still, ignoring the insect as it crawled hesitantly around the edge of the jar. But when it reached a point near the tarantula's front legs, the spider made its move.

"She just grabbed the cricket with her chelicerae," explained Mr. Verdugo. "They look like arms extending in front of her. Some people call them 'jaws' because of the poison glands inside them and the fangs at the end. Now the venom has paralyzed the cricket, and the spider can take its time to eat."

"Will she eat the whole thing?"

"She might eat the entire cricket over the next few hours, or just suck out the juices and leave the rest."

Lolo reached for the worn leather wallet he carried in his back pocket. "How much do I owe you for the cricket and gravel?" he asked.

"No charge this time. I like to see animals cared for properly and it's not often that I meet someone who shares my interest in tarantulas. What else can I do for you?"

Lolo smiled and shook his head. "Nothin' more today! You've helped me a lot! I just hope my spider likes livin' in a jar."

"Well, look at it this way. A female tarantula usually spends its entire life within a few feet of its burrow. You've already taken yours on quite a trip, and we've fed it a fat cricket, too. That's a pretty good start toward keeping a pet tarantula happy. I'm going to close up now, Lolo. It's after five-thirty. Come on back when you get a chance and we'll talk some more."

"Thanks, Mr. Verdugo," Lolo responded. "I didn't know it was so late. I gotta go, too." He picked up his tarantularium and headed for the door. "Thanks again!" he said, waving with his free hand. "I'll be back!"

4

Welcome Home

L olo hugged his tarantularium as he trudged back up the hill. Every so often he held it at arm's length to see what his new pet was doing. The red-leg had lost interest in the cricket. It remained motionless on the light blue gravel that filled the bottom of the jar.

"Aren't you hungry any more, Red-Legs? I hope you aren't scared. We're almost home."

Halfway up Geraghty Avenue he noticed his mom's yellow Toyota parked in front of their house, half on the sidewalk and half in the narrow street. He had hoped to be back from the pet store before she got home from work.

A high block wall topped with red tile and potted cactus plants partly hid the stucco-coated house. A heavy wrought-iron gate swung inward to let him into the small yard where many more plants grew—some in pots, some in the ground. A pair of banana trees next to the porch waved their yellow leaves above the edge of the tile roof.

As Lolo opened the front door, he immediately caught the aroma of hot corn tortillas.

"Mom, I'm home!" he called out. "Is dinner ready?"

"Dinner's almost ready, *m'ijo,*" Mom replied. "You are—Lolo! Get that out of here! Right now! Get that . . . thing . . . out of this house!"

Lolo hurried through the kitchen, accidentally bumping Lupita with the pickle jar as he rushed by her.

"EEEEEK!" Lupita screeched, dropping the silverware she was putting on the table. "MOM! HE HIT ME WITH IT! DO SOMETHING!"

Lolo stumbled out the back door, a look of distress on his face and Mom's words and Lupita's screams ringing in his ears. He set the tarantularium down on the small back porch, then stood for a moment, wondering if he dare go back into the house.

"Don't leave it in the backyard, Lolo!" he heard Lupita yell. "Take it away from here! We hate spiders!"

Mom opened the back door a few inches. "Lolo, you are scaring your sister with that spider! You must get rid of it!"

"But, Mom!"

"*¡Quítala de aquí! ¡Pronto!*" she said firmly. The door slammed shut.

Lolo slumped down beside the tarantularium, head bowed, arms dangling across his knees. He sat quietly for a moment, then picked up the tarantularium. He held the jar up to his face and looked inside. Once again, the cricket had the spider's attention.

"I'm sorry, Red-Legs. You can't stay here. I'm gonna have to put you in the fort for awhile." He got to his feet and carried the tarantularium over to the back fence. "It'll be okay, though. It's a great fort! The best in Las Lomitas!"

Lolo climbed through the hole in the fence and took a shortcut down the hill. When he got inside the fort, he nestled the tarantularium among the dirt clods stored under its roof.

"I'll be back as soon as I can, Red-Legs. You'll be okay!"

◆ ◆ ◆

Mom was still fuming when Lolo returned to the house. "What on earth were the two of you thinking, Papá? What if it got loose in here? I'd have to pay for an exterminator!"

"*Calmate, m'ija, no son peligrosas,*" Grandfather tried to point out.

Lolo sat down in front of a plate of chicken tostadas and rice and listened in silence as Mom and Grandfather settled the matter.

"There will be no pet spiders in or near this house! Period!"

"*Lo qué tu digas, Yolanda.* Whatever you say. *No hay problema.*"

5
Fort Araña

Lolo went down to the fort early the next morning, eager to see the tarantula he now called Red-Legs. After Mom's reaction, he had thoughts of setting Red-Legs free on the hillside or seeing if Mr. Verdugo would take her. But he couldn't make himself do either. Instead, he had decided to fix up the inside of the fort and keep Red-Legs there.

"I'm back, Red-Legs!" he said as he crawled into the fort and over to the tarantularium. He put his face next to the glass. "How you doin'? Hey, you been diggin' in the gravel, haven't you? I brought you a rock. It's bigger'n you are. I just gotta get it in there without smashin' you!"

Lolo removed the lid, then carefully lowered the chunk of shale into the jar. He set it down gently a few inches from Red-Legs. "Now you got something to hide under if you want."

As Lolo screwed the lid back on, he heard a hoarse, thinly disguised voice calling, "'Ey, you punk inside the fort! C'mon out here so I can kick your butt!"

"Hey, Frankie!" Lolo responded. "Your voice is changin'! Are you startin' to shave your ugly face, too?"

"'Ey, homes!" Frankie laughed, sticking his head through the crawl-hole. "You still alive? We thought those Record Avenue *cholos* woulda killed you by now!"

"Yeah," said Mario, entering the fort behind Frankie. "You musta got lucky!"

"I got somethin' else besides luck. C'mere and see it!"

"Geez!" exclaimed Mario, backing away.

"Where'd you get it?" Frankie asked, squinting his eyes to see better without getting too close.

"I found it after you guys left yesterday. My *abuelo* and I caught it. It's a tarantula, ya know. Mr. Verdugo at the pet store says it's a Mexican red-leg, so I call it Red-Legs."

"Is the lid on tight?" asked Mario, moving closer to the jar.

"It's not gonna hurt you, Mario," said Lolo, lifting the jar onto his lap. "Mr. Verdugo even picked it up with his bare hand!"

"Man, it looks mean!" said Frankie, coming closer. "It ain't got no face, just an ugly head with hairy things stickin' out!"

"Yeah. My sister's scared of it and my mom won't let it near the house. I'm gonna have to keep it here in the fort."

"Are you sayin' that Red-Legs is gonna be our mascot?" asked Mario, his face now close to the jar.

" 'Ey, that ain't a bad idea, homes!" said Frankie, a grin spreading across his face. "A big, ugly *araña* for a mascot! That's tough!"

"How 'bout Fort Araña?" suggested Mario in a serious tone. "It's got a tough sound to it."

"Okay with me," agreed Lolo.

"Don't mess with Fort Araña!" growled Frankie, his fist punching at no one in particular. "Yeah!"

♦ ♦ ♦

Over the next few days, Lolo spent much of his time at Fort Araña. He drew pictures of Red-Legs with the set of colored pencils and drawing paper he got for his last birthday. An old piece of carpet he found beside a neighbor's trash barrel made the floor more comfortable. A wooden berry crate from Monica's Market served as a table. He brought peaches from the tree in his backyard for snacks, and a pop bottle of water for Red-Legs and himself.

When the afternoons got too warm on the hillside, Lolo took the tarantularium over to City Terrace Park. It was always cooler in the shade of the park's tall eucalyptus trees, and a steady breeze made it even more pleasant.

Lolo liked to lie on the grass with his face close to the jar and just watch Red-Legs. When Frankie and Mario joined him, he would try to answer their questions.

"Would Red-Legs bite you if it had a chance?" Mario wanted to know.

"A tarantula doesn't bite with its mouth," Lolo explained. "It sticks fangs in you and injects venom. Its fangs are at the ends of those two things comin' out of its head. When you pick up a tarantula, you gotta keep your hand behind its head so it won't get you."

Mario had a look of concern on his face. "You aren't gonna take it out of the jar, are you?"

"No, Mario. Besides, Red-Legs likes insects a lot better than she likes you."

"What're those two things stickin' out from its back end?" Frankie asked. "They look like stingers to me."

"I'm not sure," Lolo replied. "I've been watchin' to see what she does with 'em, but I haven't seen nothin' yet. That's one of the questions I want to ask Mr. Verdugo."

♦ ♦ ♦

When almost a week had gone by since the tarantula's feeding at the pet store, the three friends, shirtless and barefooted, went grasshopper hunting along the hillside near Fort Araña.

"There goes one!" shouted Mario, pointing after a greenish blur flying away from him.

"There it goes, all right," grunted Lolo. "Right into the cactus."

"I ain't goin' after it," said Frankie. "'Bout killed my feet the last time I went in there."

"There's one on the rock behind you, Frankie!" Lolo whispered excitedly. "Don't make any fast moves!"

All three moved cautiously to surround the motionless insect.

"I can get it!" claimed Frankie in a hoarse whisper. "I'm the baddest hunter!"

As Frankie reached down to grab the grasshopper, it leaped into the air straight at Mario. Mario froze as the flying insect struck him on his bare chest, then fell stunned at his feet.

"I got it!" Mario gasped as he cupped it with both hands, then picked it up.

"I woulda got it, but you scared it!" complained Frankie.

"You scared it and I got it!" argued Mario. "I'm the baddest hunter!"

"Both of you are baa-ad hunters!" Lolo said, laughing. "Let's get the wild beast inside the fort before it escapes!"

"Can I put it in the jar, Lolo?" Frankie asked when they reached the crawl-hole.

"Mario's got the grasshopper," Lolo answered.

"I don't wanna do it," said Mario. "Here, Frankie. Take it."

When they were inside the fort, Lolo removed the tarantularium's lid, and Frankie dropped the grasshopper inside. It hopped only once, hitting the side of the jar and falling on the gravel beside Red-Legs.

"Geez, look at that!" gasped Mario when Red-Legs seized its prey.

They huddled around the tarantularium, fascinated by the helplessness of the paralyzed insect and the feeding movements of the spider. Frankie shook his head. "Man, I'd hate to be that—"

THUD! Something hit the cardboard above their heads, shaking it. Then a second THUD, and a third. Without a word between them, each grabbed a handful of dirt clods and scrambled over to the fort's front wall. They peeked over the top, then stood up together and started throwing, sending a barrage of clods in the direction of two young teenagers who laughed and gestured with their fingers as they retreated back to Record Avenue.

"It's Rogelio and that guy they call Joker!" cried Frankie, his dark, angry eyes fixed on the two attackers.

"They used rocks, too!" said Lolo, breathlessly. "Look what they did!" He pointed to the caved-in cardboard along the side of the roof.

"Did we hit either of 'em?" asked Mario.

"I don't think so," replied Lolo, "But they sure ran when we fired away at 'em."

"Fort Araña!" Frankie shouted. "*¡Ganamos! Somos los mejores!* We're the best, man!"

6

Who's Scared of What?

I got us a flagpole!" Mario announced the next morning when he arrived at the fort carrying a long bamboo pole. "I saw this in my uncle's garage, and he said I could have it. What can we use for a flag?"

Lolo and Frankie had come down early to reinforce the roof and check on Red-Legs. "We need a flag with a big, ugly araña on it," said Frankie. Then, looking at Lolo he said, "You can draw one for us, homes!"

"Can you, Lolo?" Mario asked, hopefully.

"Yeah, I might be able to. Paper won't work too good, but I can ask my mom if she has some cloth."

"Yeah, like a piece of sheet or a towel," said Mario. "I can ask my mom, too."

"I already have some drawings of Red-Legs. Maybe we can just pick the one we like best, and I can copy it on the cloth with ink. I won't see my mom, though, 'til she gets home from work."

"Me neither," said Mario. "So what're we gonna do today? Go to the park?"

"*Sí,* homeys. *¡Vamos al parque!*" answered Frankie.

"Let's take a basketball with us," said Lolo. "Does yours have air in it, Frankie?"

"Yeah, mine's got air. You gonna teach your *araña* how to shoot baskets?"

"Not this time. I'm still tryin' to teach you! Let's go get the ball."

"Let's go by Monica's, too," said Mario. "I've got money for a soda."

Lolo headed up the hill with the tarantularium tucked under his arm. Frankie and Mario were right behind him. They cut through Lolo's yard to get to Geraghty Avenue, got the ball at Frankie's house, and went on to Monica's Market.

The little grocery store had been part of this hilly neighborhood of narrow streets and modest frame houses for as long as most people could remember. Its cement block walls extended above its flat, asphalt roof. They were coated with plaster and painted white to looked like adobe. Wall air-conditioning units worked at keeping it cool inside, while a ceiling fan above the always-open front entrance chased away flies and summer heat. Monica was the latest of several owners.

"I'm gonna stay out here with Red-Legs," Lolo said when they reached the entrance. "Tell Monica I'm out here with my tarantula, if she wants to see it."

Frankie and Mario went on in. A moment later, Lolo could hear Monica's reply himself.

"I don't think Monica likes spiders," Mario said as he came out of the store with a two-liter bottle of orange soda cradled in his arm. He grinned at Lolo. "Frankie told her that you have your tarantula on a rope 'cause it's too big to fit in the jar she gave you. She went crazy, man!"

Frankie tried to look innocent as he sauntered out with the basketball under his arm, but his wide grin gave him away. "She flipped out, homes! Did you hear all those bad words?"

Lolo shook his head. "I don't understand women! They get scared over nothin'!"

♦ ♦ ♦

City Terrace Park was over on Hazard Avenue several blocks away from Monica's by car, but only the length of a football field by hiking across a brush-covered ravine and a vacant lot. Kids from all over Las Lomitas came to swim in the pool, or play on the diamonds and courts.

"There's a half-court we can use," Mario pointed out. "We can put Red-Legs and our drink in the shade of that tree near the backboard."

Frankie took some shots while Lolo and Mario

set the tarantularium and pop bottle on the shaded grass. "'Ey, homeys! Look who's comin'," he said as they joined Frankie on the court. He nodded in the direction of two girls walking along the edge of the courts toward them.

"It's Lisa Gomez!" whispered Mario. "She was in our class last year."

"And you were in love with her, 'ey Mario?"

"So were you, Frankie," Mario snapped.

"So was everybody, homes. Right, Lolo?"

"That's her sister Leticia with her," Lolo responded, ignoring the question. "They sure look like sisters."

Both girls had long black hair pulled back in swishy pony tails, and large brown eyes that sparkled when they smiled. They looked like twins in their navy blue shorts, sleeveless white blouses, and red-and-white tennis shoes. As they got closer, the taller one called out, "Hi, Frankie! Hi, Mario! Hi, Lolo!"

"How you doin', *chicas?*" Frankie answered as the girls joined them.

"Hi, Lisa," mumbled Mario, his eyes avoiding hers.

"Hi," was all Lolo said.

Lisa smiled sweetly. "Are you guys having a good game?"

"We just got here," said Mario, more confidently.

"We're gonna show Lolo's *araña* how to shoot

baskets," boasted Frankie. He turned toward the tarantularium. "It's gonna like my hook shot."

Lisa looked curiously at the jar, then walked over to it. "Come look, Leticia! It's a tarantula!"

As they all gathered around the tarantularium, Lisa asked, "Is this really yours, Lolo?" When Lolo nodded, she exclaimed, "I love its colors!"

Lolo stared at her in surprise. "It's a girl. I named her Red-Legs."

"Oh, how cute! Can I hold Red-Legs, Lolo?"

Everyone looked at Lolo. His face flushed and his eyes shifted nervously. "Better not today," he finally stammered. "She's still a little scared of people."

"Some other time, I hope. Will you be bringing it to school?"

"Maybe. I'll think about it."

"Just one more week," Lisa said. "I hope we're in the same class!"

"Yea," was all Lolo could say.

Lisa smiled at him and said, "I gotta go. C'mon, Leticia. Bye, you guys!"

The boys stood quietly for a moment until Lisa and Leticia were out of earshot. "Wow!" Mario's voice was respectful. "She wants to hold the tarantula!"

Frankie shook his head, "She's *loca en la cabeza.*"

Lolo's mind was racing. "Let's go ahead and shoot a few, then I've gotta get goin'."

"Where you gotta go, homes?"

"I'm gonna go back to the pet store. I need to talk to Mr. Verdugo again. Go ahead, Frankie. Shoot!"

7
Spiderphobia

Animales Domésticos was an old, red-brick building that once housed two small stores. The first entrance Lolo came to was closed and locked. Its window display areas provided storage space for stacks of pet food bags and empty cages and terrariums. A sign on the door read, Enter By The Other Door/*Entrada Por La Otra Puerta,* with an arrow pointing to the left. The windows of the real entrance displayed a litter of sleepy-eyed puppies on one side, and an exhibit of aquarium supplies on the other. Inside the store, Mr. Verdugo was stocking shelves with bird care items when he saw Lolo enter carrying the tarantularium.

"*Hola,* Lolo. I've been thinking about you and your red-leg. How are you both doing?"

"We're okay, Mr. Verdugo. Red-Legs ate a grasshopper yesterday and I think she likes her tarantularium. She digs in the gravel."

Mr. Verdugo adjusted his glasses before taking the jar from Lolo. "She looks fine. Her hairs have a healthy shine to them, and she's moving about okay."

"What're those two little things stickin' out her back end?" Lolo asked, remembering Frankie's question.

"Those are spinnerets. She uses them to lay out the silk her body makes for webbing."

"Do tarantula spiders make spider webs?"

Mr. Verdugo set the jar on the counter in front of him. "Not the kind the other spiders weave to catch flying insects. Burrowing tarantulas line their burrows with webbing. They also spin a blanket of silk for their eggs, and for lying on during molting."

A puzzled frown came over Lolo's face. "What's molting?"

"That's when they shed old skin that's been replaced with new skin. Older tarantulas molt at least once a year. Younger ones do it more often."

"Will a tarantula hurt you if it sticks you with its fangs?"

"It's a lot like a bee sting. It hurts, but it's not serious unless a person is allergic to it."

"Would you show me how to pick up Red-Legs?" Lolo asked in a different, more tense voice.

"Sure! You can take her out of the tarantularium."

Mr. Verdugo unscrewed the jar's lid. "Just reach down and take hold on each side of her front body section. Your thumb and index finger should go between a middle pair of legs. Pin her down—not too hard, but hold firm. Then, lift her so that all eight legs come up at the same time. Go ahead, now. You can set her down in that plastic tray."

Lolo hesitated for a moment, then placed his right hand inside the jar. He slowly lowered it to within a couple of inches of Red-Legs. Lolo swallowed hard, a look of anguish on his face. "I can't do it," he whispered, pulling his hand back out.

"That's okay!" said Mr. Verdugo, reassuringly. "Let me show you."

He lowered his hand into the jar and grasped Red-Legs firmly with his thumb and forefinger. He held her still, then lifted her straight up and out. "Red-Legs feels very insecure right now," he said. "If just one claw grabbed hold of anything, she would start to struggle and could hurt herself." He set Red-Legs down in the tray. "There's another way to pick up a tarantula," he continued. "You might find this easier."

"I'll try it," responded Lolo, trying to sound confident. "I get scared that she might bite!"

"I understand, Lolo. It's scary for most people. Now just put the palm of your hand in front of

Red-Legs. You're going to give her a little push from behind with your other hand. She'll walk right onto your palm and just sit there."

"You're sure she won't bite me instead?"

"There are no guarantees, Lolo, but the chances are she won't. Don't do it if you don't want to."

Lolo placed the back of his left hand on the surface of the tray, then slowly moved it closer to Red-Legs. His right hand trembled as he brought it down behind her. He took a deep breath before gently nudging her spinnerets. The tarantula moved sluggishly forward, its front legs reaching toward the outstretched palm. At the first touch of the spider, Lolo jerked his hand away, then stepped back from the counter, head bowed. He blinked away tears forming in his eyes. "Sorry, Mr. Verdugo," he said, his voice choked.

"Don't worry about it, Lolo. You've just got a touch of spiderphobia. A tarantula owner should be able to handle his pet, but only when necessary. There's always the danger that the spider could be accidentally dropped and that could kill it. Take it easy on yourself. *Suavecito.*"

"Thanks, Mr. Verdugo. You've taught me a lot."

"*De nada, mi amigo.* By the way, I'm taking my tarantulas to the county fair in about a week. Would you let me take your red-leg along with them?"

The request took Lolo completely by surprise.

"Where's that?" were all the words he could find for the moment.

"The fairgrounds are in Pomona. That's a city east of here about twenty miles. It's still in Los Angeles County, though. It's the Los Angeles County Fair. I'm going to take the tarantulas over there on Thursday of next week. That's the day it opens. They'll stay there with my sister for the two-and-a-half weeks of the fair. You and I can go over on Sundays to check on them, and to see the fair, too. What do you think?"

"Man! I'd like that! I've never seen a fair. What's it like?"

"Lots of exhibits. Everything from pigs, goats, and fancy birds, to arts and crafts. There's horse racing, bands, clowns, carnival rides, and all kinds of food."

Lolo's eyes shone with excitement. "I wanna go!" he said. "Red-Legs does too, I'll bet!" he added with a grin.

Mr. Verdugo smiled. "It will be good for both of you to get away from your 'burrows' and see what some of the rest of the world is like. Talk to your folks about what I've said, Lolo, and let me know what they say."

"I will, Mr. Verdugo. School starts on Monday. I'll come by on my way home."

"*Bueno*, Lolo. I'll see you then."

8

Hazardous Hazard

"Why would anybody take spiders to a county fair?" Mom asked that evening when Lolo told her of Mr. Verdugo's invitation. "It sounds pretty strange to me. How does it sound to you, Papá?"

"*No sé,* Yolanda," replied Grandfather. "*Tal vez es mejor si tú hablas con el Señor Verdugo.* Ask him."

"I think I will," Mom decided. "I'll go by his shop tomorrow on my way home from work. Then, Lolo, I'll let you know whether you can go to the fair or not. As far as your tarantula is concerned, *m'ijo,* that's up to you."

◆ ◆ ◆

"Man, you're lucky!" said Mario when Lolo told him and Frankie about the county fair invitation. The three had met at the fort early to play, and to build up their pile of dirt clods.

"'Ey, Lolo, do ya think you could get Mr. Verdugo

to take us, too?" Frankie asked hopefully. "I ain't been outta East L.A. in my whole life, 'cept the time we went to my tía's in Baldwin Park."

"I've been to San Diego and Tijuana," boasted Mario, "but not to a fair. Do ya think he would, Lolo?"

Lolo hesitated, doubtful. "I dunno. I guess I could ask. It'd be great if we could all go." Then he added wistfully, "I've never been anywhere either."

"What else did he say, homes? You sure moved your butt in a hurry for somethin'!"

"I just needed to know some things about Red-Legs, that's all. No big deal." Then he quickly changed the subject. "Do you guys wanna go over to the school?"

"What for, homes?"

"We can find out what class we're in. The lists should be up by now."

"I hope we're in the same class again," said Mario.

"Who, you and Lisa?" Frankie teased.

"Shut up, Frankie!"

"C'mon you guys," Lolo cut in. "Let's get our bikes and go Hazardous."

◆ ◆ ◆

Bike riding in Las Lomitas had its ups and downs. The ups tested strong legs against steep hills, with the hills often winning. The downs were the next best thing to flying. Lolo's house was about halfway up into Las Lomitas. "All the way up" meant a leg-cramping pump further on to City Terrace Drive. Though in the opposite direction from school, the reward was "Hazardous Hazard," the long, downhill stretch of Hazard Avenue from City Terrace Drive all the way to Hammel Street and the school.

They rested their bikes in the shade of a towering eucalyptus tree at the top of Hazard. Lolo rode an old Sting Ray his mom had bought at a yard sale four years ago. He had it stripped down the way he liked it and painted the frame black. Frankie's bike was a long, low original made from pieces and parts he had traded for or found. It was heavier than a Stingray, and hard to beat going downhill. Mario owned a new BMX that he'd gotten last Christmas. He worried so much about someone stealing it that he kept it in his bedroom most of the time.

"The last time me and Mario were up here, two big dudes tried to jump us," Frankie remarked. "'Member that, Mario?"

"Yeah, after you mouthed-off to them first, Frankie. Then they called us a bunch of names, and threw stuff at us." Mario looked around nervously. "We split real fast."

"Well, let's do the same thing," said Lolo, pushing off. "Real fast!"

They headed down the steepest part of Hazard in loose formation, three abreast. Picking up speed in no time, they sailed along in the middle of the street until an oncoming car forced them to edge over to the right. By this time, Frankie had taken the lead, with Lolo right behind him and Mario a close third. The buffeting breeze made their eyes water and their hair stand at attention above their foreheads. They sat tall, sometimes no hands, fast and cool.

The street leveled off as they approached City Terrace Park. Frankie called out, "Look what's happenin'!" and pointed to two boys leaving the park and walking down Hazard, their backs to the bike riders.

"Rogelio and Joker!" Lolo called back.

"Right!" yelled Frankie. "Check this out!"

Pumping now to increase speed, Frankie swooped down on his target like a hawk after its prey. His target was the black cap worn backwards on Joker's shaved head, its bill shading the back of his neck.

"HEY, WHAT THE . . . !" a startled Joker exploded as Frankie flashed by and the cap flew off. "HEY! YOU PUNK!"

Frankie had tried to pluck the cap from Joker's head, but knocked it off instead. The effort cost him his balance, and his bike swerved out of control toward the left side of the street.

"Watch out, Frankie!" Lolo yelled behind him, skidding his bike to a stop before nearly crashing into him. Frankie hit the dirt along the street's shoulder as his bike slammed into the front of a parked car.

"I'M GONNA GETCHA PUNK!" bellowed Joker, charging toward the fallen cap snatcher.

Hearing those words, Frankie scrambled to his feet, took one look at his broken bike, and ran to Lolo. "I'm gettin' on, homes!"

Lolo scooted forward on his bike's banana seat, and Frankie jumped on behind him.

"GO, MAN!" Frankie screamed.

Lolo stood on the pedals and Frankie pushed asphalt with his feet. They could hear Joker panting and swearing as he raced to within spitting distance of the Stingray's back tire.

"GO, HOMEY!"

Lolo pumped as hard and fast as he could, maintaining the short distance between them and the onrushing Joker, then gradually pulling away.

"I'M GONNA . . . GETCHOO . . . PUNKS!" Joker hollered one more time before giving up the chase, red-faced and gasping for breath.

"Okay if I wet my pants, homes?" Frankie hollered in Lolo's ear.

"Not on my bike!" Lolo hollered back.

"Just kiddin', man! 'Ey, there's Mario waitin' for us."

"Let's get outta here!" Mario demanded when the pair pulled alongside him and rocks ricocheted near them.

"Where ya been, Mario? You missed the action, man!"

"I didn't miss nothin'!" snapped Mario, taking the lead and not looking back.

Hazard sloped downward again and the bikes picked up speed. The descent was gradual, though, and they glided along easily.

"Whatcha gonna do about your bike, Frankie?" Lolo asked over his shoulder.

"Aah, no sweat. I'll get it later. It's busted up pretty bad. Nobody's gonna ride it."

"Still wanna go to the school?"

"Yeah. That's better'n any place else right now."

9
Someone New
in 202

H ammel Street School looked like two brick-red lunch boxes side-by-side facing Brannick Avenue, a short, dead-end street off of Hammel. Students entered the classrooms through central hallways that were parallel to Brannick. There was a courtyard between the two-story brick buildings. A tall, silvery flagpole marked the center of the courtyard. Rows of bicycle racks stood upright near the building entrance on the left.

"Let's lock our bikes together with my chain, Lolo. Nobody would want my bike if they had to take yours, too."

"You're funny as spit, Mario. I'll lock my own bike."

"No fightin', homeys! It's against the rules at Hammel Street School," Frankie advised in mock seriousness.

"You should know," countered Mario. "You've got the record here for breakin' that rule."

"Not me-ee!" Frankie declared, a look of wide-eyed innocence on his battle-scarred face. "You're thinkin' of—"

Lolo didn't let him finish. "Are you guys comin'? The lists are in the office."

"Oh, yeah! The lists!" said Frankie. "What lucky teacher is gonna get us?"

They found the class lists posted on a hallway bulletin board outside the open office door. Mrs. Martinez, the school secretary, called to them from behind the office counter. "Hello, boys! Welcome back!"

"Hi, Mrs. Martinez," Lolo said in return. Frankie and Mario echoed him. "Are our names here?"

"They should be, Lolo. Let's see if I can help you."

She stepped around the counter just as Mario found his name. "Here's my name on Mr. Baca's list . . . and here's yours, too, Frankie."

Frankie shrugged his shoulders. "That's cool," he said. "Mr. Baca's okay. What about you, Lolo? Ain't we stickin' together?"

"Here's your name, Lolo." Mrs. Martinez placed her finger on another list. "You're with one of our new teachers, Miss Hernandez. She's very nice. You'll like her class."

The boys looked at where she was pointing. Mario's staring eyes fixed themselves on the name below Lolo's. "Lisa's in your class!" he blurted out, then caught himself, embarrassed.

"'Ey, homes, lucky you!" said Frankie.

Lolo flushed in silence.

"Miss Hernandez is here today, Lolo, if you'd like to meet her. She should be working in her room—second floor, 202."

"Thanks, Mrs. Martinez. You guys wanna come with me?"

"Sure," replied Mario.

"Yeah," said Frankie. "Let's check out the new teacher."

The stairs to the second floor were next to the office. The boys raced up them two steps at a time, something they weren't allowed to do when school was in session. They skidded to a stop outside room 202. Lolo pulled the door open a few inches and peeked inside.

The young teacher, dressed casually in faded jeans and a yellow short-sleeved blouse, was standing on a chair behind her desk. She stretched on her tiptoes each time she stapled a card to the wall high above the chalkboard. Lolo noticed that her jet-black hair was braided in two braids, looped up behind her ears like his mom often did with hers. She turned to look at him as he stepped into the room.

"Hi! You're just in time! Could you get me that card I dropped?" She pointed to the floor near her desk. Frankie and Mario came in behind Lolo as he went to get the card. He turned it over to see the letter *S* in manuscript and cursive, capital and lowercase.

"Thanks. I'm tired of getting down off this chair only to climb back on it again." She stapled the card Lolo handed her, then turned to him again. "What's your name?"

"I'm Lolo Garcia. I'm gonna be in your class."

"Well, that's great! I'm Miss Hernandez. Are these two your friends?"

"Yes, Miss Hernandez. This is Frankie and that's Mario."

"We're in Mr. Baca's class," Mario said importantly.

Miss Hernandez stepped down from the chair. "I haven't met Mr. Baca yet. This is just my second day. How do you boys like it here at Hammel?"

Frankie laughed. "It's okay when I'm not busted for somethin'!"

"I like it," said Mario. "Especially math."

"What about you, Lolo?"

"It's okay," he said without enthusiasm. "I do best in art."

"You gonna tell her 'bout your araña?" asked Frankie.

"You have a spider, Lolo?"

"She's a tarantula. I named her Red-Legs 'cause it's a Mexican red-leg."

"I'd love to see it!" Her voice was sincere. "Can you bring it to school?"

A smile brightened Lolo's face.

"We'll be studying about living things during the first quarter," Miss Hernandez continued. "Everything from single-cell plants and animals to redwood trees and whales. I want our classroom to be filled with lots of examples. Your tarantula would be perfect!"

Lolo continued to beam. "I could bring her!" he said cheerfully. "But not 'til she comes back from the fair."

"You're taking your tarantula to a fair?" Miss Hernandez asked, a puzzled look on her face.

"Mr. Verdugo from the pet store is taking Red-Legs next week," Lolo replied. "He's taking his tarantulas, too."

Mario tried to clarify. "It's called the Los Angeles Fair."

"Oh, the county fair!" Miss Hernandez concluded.

"Yeah, that's it," said Lolo. "I get to go over there on Sundays!"

"We might go, too!" said Frankie.

"That's wonderful for all of you! I hope you'll tell me all about it when you bring Red-Legs."

"I will!" Lolo promised, his smile widening.

"Good for you, Lolo! Right now, though, I need to get back to work. If you boys want to stay, I can put you to work, too."

The three exchanged looks. "I better go home," said Mario. "It's way past lunchtime and my mom worries."

"I guess we better all go," said Lolo. "Maybe I can help you some other time, Miss Hernandez."

"Thank you, Lolo. You all have a pleasant weekend, and I'll see you on Monday!"

"Bye, teacher," said Mario.

"Adiós, maestra," said Frankie.

"Bye, Miss Hernandez," said Lolo. "See you Monday!"

10

Fair or No Fair?

L et's stop at the pet store for a minute," Lolo
said, unchaining his bike. "I wanna tell Mr.
Verdugo that my mom is comin' over later."

"You wanna ask him 'bout me and Mario goin' to
the fair?" Frankie urged.

"Yeah, I will," Lolo replied. "But what if he says
yes about you goin' and my mom says no about me
goin'?"

"Then we'll tell you all about it when we get
back," said Mario, grinning.

"That's real funny, Mario. . . . 'bout as funny as
spit. I'll laugh when I have time."

"He's just kiddin', Lolo," Frankie said soothingly.
"We wanna all three go."

◆ ◆ ◆

The ride to Animales Domésticos took less than
five minutes. This time, Lolo and Mario chained
their bikes together, then the three entered the

store. Several people were browsing while Mr. Verdugo sold a hamster to a woman and her little girl, so the boys looked around, too.

"Geez! Look at that python!" Mario said, pointing at a large glass cage. "I never saw one that big before!"

"Watch out, Mario," Lolo warned. "It's big enough to swallow you."

"Then it wouldn't ever have to eat again, 'ey homes."

"Shut up, Frankie!"

"Hey, you guys, here comes Mr. Verdugo," Lolo whispered. "Don't be messin' around."

"Hi, Lolo. How many snakes can I sell you boys today?"

"We're not buyin' snakes, Mr. Verdugo. I just wanted to tell you that my mom is comin' by to talk to you when she gets off work today. Then she'll tell me if I can go to the fair."

"Great! I'll tell her all about it."

"These are my friends Frankie and Mario. I was wonderin' if they could go to the fair with us if my mom says it's okay for me."

Frankie and Mario stood quietly, looking up at Mr. Verdugo. He looked back at them and smiled. "That's fine with me. Would you boys like to go to the county fair with us?"

"Yeah! I would!" blurted Frankie.

"Me, too!" sang Mario.

"Then you'll have to get your parents' permission, too. Just have them call me or come by the shop."

"Thanks, Mr. Verdugo!" said Lolo.

"Yeah, thanks!" said Frankie and Mario at the same time, flush-faced and happy.

"That's a week from Sunday," Mr. Verdugo reminded them. "And I'll be taking the tarantulas over Thursday afternoon, Lolo."

"Okay, Mr. Verdugo."

"I've got customers waiting, so I'll see you boys later."

♦ ♦ ♦

The three left the store as happy and playful as the puppies in the window.

"All right!" shouted Frankie. "We're goin' to the fair!"

"Goin' to the fair!" sang Mario.

"Goin' to the fair!" Lolo joined in.

They continued their whooping as they rode towards Las Lomitas. When they reached the foot of Geraghty Avenue, they got off the bikes and walked.

"Let's go on down to the fort," Lolo suggested. "We can look for another grasshopper for Red-Legs, and toss a few clods."

"I'm gonna get somethin' to eat first," said Mario, stopping in front of his house. "Then I might come."

"Catch you later then, Mario. How 'bout you, Frankie?"

"I gotta feed my dogs and do some other stuff and I gotta get my bike. Maybe one of my brothers'll go with me."

Frankie waved as Lolo opened the gate to his own yard. "Later, homes!"

"Later, Frankie!"

Lolo parked his bike on the porch and entered the house. "I'm home, *Abuelo.*"

Grandfather looked up from his newspaper. *"!Hola m'ijo! ¿De dónde vienes?"*

"At school with Frankie and Mario. We met my new teacher and went by the pet store. Is there anything to eat?"

"We already ate, *m'ijo. Pero hay duraznos frescos.*

Lolo went into the kitchen, took a large, ripe peach from the bowl on the table, and headed for the back door.

"I'm goin' down to the fort, *Abuelo!"* he called out.

"Está bien, m'ijo," came the reply as the door closed behind him.

♦ ♦ ♦

Something was wrong. Lolo knew it as soon as he started down the hill. The fort didn't look right. As he got closer, he realized why. Its roof was gone. The large piece of cardboard lay on the ground further down the hill, almost to Record Avenue, and the front wall had been pushed over. Boards and cement blocks were scattered down the hill. Lolo approached the fort cautiously, afraid of what else he might find. The old carpet and the box table were still there, but—a soft moan came from deep inside him—the tarantularium was gone.

"There it is!" Lolo said in a choked voice. A few feet away were the broken remains of the pickle jar mixed with blue aquarium gravel. He rushed over to look for Red-Legs, expecting to find her crushed body in the breakage. She wasn't there.

Through his eyes filled with tears, Lolo searched the hillside for his tarantula. He lifted up pieces of cardboard and wood that littered the area. He looked under bushes and large rocks. He peered into a dozen holes in the ground. There wasn't a trace of his pet.

11
Who's to Blame?

When Mom got home, she found Lolo lying on his bed in the small room he shared with Grandfather. "*M'ijo!* I met Alex Verdugo a little while ago! He's such a nice man. And what a coincidence! His sister and I went to Garfield High at the same time! She has her own business now. . . . a jewelry and gift shop down on First Street. She's going to sell some of her things at the county fair. That's where the tarantulas are going to be—attracting attention to her displays of jewelry!"

"I don't have a tarantula any more," Lolo said softly, fighting to hold back tears.

"What do you mean, Lolo?"

"Red-Legs is gone, mom. Somebody wrecked the fort and broke the tarantularium. I don't know what happened to her. They either let her go or stole her, or maybe killed her. Anyway, she's gone. We can forget the fair." He turned over and hid his face in the pillow. "It's no big deal anyway," he sobbed.

Mom sat down on the edge of the bed and rubbed Lolo's back for a few minutes without saying anything. Then she kissed the back of his neck and stood up. "I'm going to fix dinner now, *m'ijo.* I'll call you when it's ready—your favorite, *chiles rellenos.*"

"I'm not hungry," Lolo said, his voice muffled by the pillow.

◆ ◆ ◆

Lolo was up and outside at dawn the next morning, which was unusual for him on a Saturday. A gentle breeze of cool air greeted him, though the early rays of the sun gave hint to another scorcher ahead. He welcomed the peacefulness of the hillside. Only the coo-cooing of doves and the occasional crowing of a rooster broke the silence of his surroundings.

Fort Araña, desolate and abandoned, marred the landscape. Lolo walked slowly around the ruins in ever-widening circles, his eyes fixed intently on the ground so that nothing could escape his scrutiny. Now and then, a black stink-bug beetle crawled across his path, or a grasshopper hopped out of his way. But there was no sign of Red-Legs.

Almost an hour went by before he gave up and went over to the fort. He picked up dirt clods from the stockpile, leaned against the exposed back wall, and tossed them one at a time down the slope until Grandfather's whistle called him home for breakfast.

◆ ◆ ◆

"Frankie and Mario are at the back door, Lolo!" Mom called from the kitchen a little while later. Lolo came out of his bedroom without answering and headed for the service porch. He opened the door to find his two friends gazing up at him with concerned eyes.

"We been down to the fort, Lolo. Do you have the *araña?*" Frankie asked anxiously.

"No. I couldn't find her. Only the broken jar."

"Geez! I knew there'd be trouble! I knew it!" stormed Mario.

"What d'ya mean, Mario?" asked Lolo.

"He means Joker, homes. He thinks Joker's gettin' back at me for grabbin' his stupid cap."

"It was stupid to grab the stupid cap!" fumed Mario, glaring at Frankie.

Frankie didn't respond. He just stood there on the porch, hands jammed deep in the pockets of his tattered jeans, head bowed.

"It probably was Joker," said Lolo solemnly. He stepped onto the porch, and the three of them crossed the yard to the back fence.

"We can't prove it, though," Mario grumbled, "and we can't go to the fair without Red-Legs."

A look of annoyance crossed Lolo's face. "There's

more to havin' Red-Legs than goin' to a fair," he countered.

They stood silently, looking out upon the sun-browned hillside.

"Sorry, homeys," Frankie mumbled, head bowed again.

"It's not your fault, Frankie," Lolo said. "You didn't wreck the fort or do anything with Red-Legs."

"What are we gonna do now?" asked Mario, still upset.

"I dunno," Lolo admitted.

"When are you gonna tell Mr. Verdugo?"

"I dunno that either, Mario."

"What're ya gonna say to your teacher on Monday?"

"Mario, shut up for awhile! I don't know nothin' right now. I might not even go to school Monday. Let's just forget it!"

"I'm leavin' then!" snapped Mario, stomping off toward the side of the house.

"I gotta go help my mom get groceries in a few minutes, Frankie."

"Okay, Lolo. I'm outta here, too. Will you ride me to school on Monday?"

"Yeah, I guess. See you, Frankie."

"Later, homes. Sorry!"

12
Blue Monday

Lolo, Frankie, and Mario arrived at school extra early and joined the game of Butts Up that was already going on at one of the handball courts. When the bell rang, they headed for the courtyard between the two main buildings where they were to line up with their new classes. Frankie and Mario spotted tall Mr. Baca right away, and joined the students forming a double line in front of him. Lolo continued his search for Miss Hernandez.

"Over here, Lolo!" he heard a girl's voice calling to him. He saw a hand waving and caught a glimpse of a pretty face through the crowd. It was Lisa Gomez.

"Hi, Lolo!" she said when he reached her and the other students standing with Miss Hernandez. "This is our class!"

"Hi, Lisa," Lolo replied. "I didn't see you at first."

"I'm glad we're in the same class!" She said without

shyness, her eyes sparkling as she smiled. "Maybe we can study about tarantulas together. How is Red-Legs doing?"

"I don't have Red-Legs anymore," Lolo responded solemnly. "Somebody wrecked the place where I kept her and smashed her tarantularium. I don't know what happened to her."

Lisa's smile disappeared and her eyes blinked back tears. "I'm sorry, Lolo! I'm so sorry!"

Lolo flushed, not knowing what more to say. "It's no big deal," he finally mumbled as the principal's voice came over the public address system.

After the flag salute and announcements, the classes marched off to their rooms. Miss Hernandez led her students to the door of room 202, then stood to one side to greet them individually as they entered. When Lolo's turn came, she smiled warmly at him and said, "Lolo, I haven't forgotten about you and your tarantula!"

"Hello, Miss Hernandez," was all Lolo could bring himself to say. He went on in and found his name tag on the desk in front of Lisa's. He slumped into the seat, wishing he could go home right now and check the hillside again.

Room 202 was much cheerier than Lolo's mood. The classroom caught the morning sun through tall three-tiered windows that overlooked the blacktop playground. Fresh paint gleamed from walls and woodwork, and the hardwood floors glistened with new wax. Miss Hernandez had decorated the bulletin boards with colorful pictures and trimmings, and the custodian had washed all traces of chalk dust from the black slate chalkboards. All of this was lost on Lolo. Only one thing was on his mind.

Miss Hernandez got the class off to a fast start with a math lesson. Lolo's attention wandered back and forth between her words and his thought of Red-Legs. "I have to find out what happened to her!" he said aloud, softly.

Miss Hernandez paused and looked at him. "Do you have a question, Lolo?" she asked pleasantly.

Lolo flushed, his face burning with embarrassment. "No, teacher," he said swallowing hard. "Excuse me."

Lolo tried to pay attention during the rest of the lesson, but it wasn't until Miss Hernandez changed the subject that he really began to listen.

"Let's talk about science projects for a few minutes," he heard her say. "As we begin our study of living things, I want each of you to think about the plant or animal you'd like to choose as your special subject. You will research that subject and present an oral report to the class sometime next month. Include live examples, if possible, or pictures or drawings."

"Can we work in partners, Miss Hernandez?"

someone in the front row asked.

"Partners are okay as long as both do their share of the work. By the way, subjects already chosen by some of you who dropped by last week are guinea pigs, sunflowers, and tarantulas."

Lolo scrunched down in his seat at the mention of tarantulas, carefully avoiding eye contact with Miss Hernandez. It didn't do any good.

"Lolo," she said and turned to face him, smiling. "Would you like to tell the class where your tarantula will be going this week?"

Lolo reddened again as everyone looked at him. "I don't have a tarantula anymore," he said in a firm but quiet voice. "Somebody stole her or killed her."

Murmurs of concern came from other students. Miss Hernandez stepped closer to Lolo, her deep brown eyes kind and questioning. "That's terrible, Lolo! Who would do such a thing?"

"That's what I wanna find out," he replied firmly.

"Could we talk about this after school, Lolo?" Miss Hernandez asked softly.

Lolo shifted uncomfortably in his seat. "I . . . I can't today," he said awkwardly. "I gotta . . . there's somethin' I gotta do."

Miss Hernandez smiled understandingly. "Perhaps another time, Lolo."

♦ ♦ ♦

After school, Lolo went by himself to Animales Domésticos. Mr. Verdugo was waiting on a customer, but he waved to Lolo and pointed to a display case on Lolo's right. Lolo looked at the case, his eyes widening. There, lined up along the top of the glass counter, were four small terrariums that had been converted into tarantulariums. Each had a small sign taped to its glass.

"Texas cinnamon," Lolo read aloud as he approached the first one. Partly hidden under a rock was a small, yellowish-red tarantula. It remained perfectly still as Lolo stuck his face up close to the glass to get a better look. "You are a lot like Red-Legs except for your color," Lolo said aloud. "And your size," he continued. "Red-Legs is a lot bigger than you."

He moved over to the next tarantularium. "Man! Look at you!" The black tarantula he was staring at was huge, much bigger than Red-Legs. The spider's complete blackness made it look dangerous. It had hooks so he knew it was a male. The sign on its home identified it as a Honduran black velvet. "You do look as soft as velvet," Lolo said to him, "but I don't wanna touch you."

The third tarantula, a Mexican brown, was walking around the perimeter of its glass box as if looking for a way out. It, too, was smaller than Red-Legs. Lolo noticed that half of one of its front legs was missing.

The sign on the fourth tarantularium read Mexican red-leg. Lolo knew that this one was empty. He turned away from it as his sadness brought tears to his eyes.

"Well, Thursday is the big day for our tarantulas!" Mr. Verdugo said cheerfully as he joined Lolo. "I fixed up a tarantularium for yours so that they'll all be the same. You can keep it when the fair is over."

"I . . . I don't . . . have Red-Legs any more," Lolo replied.

Mr. Verdugo's brow wrinkled in a frown. "What happened?"

"Somebody wrecked our fort where I kept Red-Legs. They smashed the pickle jar, and now Red-Legs is gone. I'm sorry, Mr. Verdugo."

"Oh, man! I'm sorry, too, Lolo. I know that Red-Legs means a lot to you. Any idea who did it?"

"It might'a been a couple teenage guys gettin' back at us for somethin' . . . but I dunno for sure."

"Do you suppose they took Red-Legs, and you might be able to get her back?"

Lolo thought for a moment. "Maybe, but . . . why would they break the pickle jar if they wanted to take her?"

"Good point," agreed Mr. Verdugo. "Would you like me to get another tarantula for you? It could be delivered in a few days."

Lolo wiped his eyes with the back of his hand. "Thanks anyway, Mr. Verdugo. I don't want another tarantula. I'd better go now. I came by to tell you what happened."

"Come back soon, Lolo. Sorry about Red-Legs."

13
Dead or Alive?

*T*he cafeteria menu for the second day of school featured Salisbury steak and mashed potatoes, Lolo's favorite. "Can I have some extra gravy, please?" he asked the student server. "And some more of those little mushrooms, too?" he added.

"He can have mine, chica," Frankie offered as he came up behind Lolo. "I hate gravy! Salsa *sí*, gravy no is what I always say."

"Let's sit over there," said Lolo, nodding in the direction of an almost-empty table. "We've got some heavy thinkin' to do."

Mario caught up with them as they were sitting down. "Are we gonna talk about Red-Legs again?" he asked cautiously, setting his tray across from Lolo's.

"We gotta figure a way to check out Joker to see if he's got Red-Legs, or if he killed her," Lolo began.

"Without gettin' killed ourselves, I hope," interrupted Mario.

Lolo shrugged his shoulders. "First we gotta find out where Joker lives."

"He must be kinda new 'round here," said Frankie. "My brothers don't know 'um."

"We know he hangs with Rogelio a lot," said Lolo. "We could look for 'um on Record or at the park, then follow 'um."

"Geez!" exploded Mario, his pudgy face turning red. "So now we're gonna be a buncha detectives? How can we follow him without gettin' caught?"

Frankie's eyes narrowed as he smacked his right fist into the palm of his left hand. "We should just kick their butts!" he growled. "I can get my brothers to help us and we'll kick some butt!"

"C'mon, Frankie, get serious," said Lolo.

"I am serious, homes!" said Frankie, smacking his fist again. Then his face broke into a wide grin. "Serious 'bout givin' Mario a hard time." He chuckled, "Right, Mario?"

Mario glared at Frankie but said nothing.

"'Ey, Lolo. Here comes Lisa," observed Frankie. "I think she likes you, man!"

Lolo turned to see Lisa approaching their table, her eyes on them and a pretty smile on her face. "Hi, Lolo. Hi, Frankie. Hi, Mario," she greeted them.

"Hi, Lisa," all three responded in unison.

"How you been, chica?" Frankie asked.

"Fine, Frankie, thanks . . . except I'm still wondering about Red-Legs."

"We been talkin' about that," said Lolo. "We're tryin' to figure out what to do to find out if someone's got her, or if she's dead."

"So far, Frankie's got us committin' suicide to find out," blurted Mario, his agitation still showing.

"You ever hear of a dude they call Joker?" Frankie asked, his eyebrows raised.

Lisa thought for a moment. "Oh, yeah. That's Richie Rios. He's in eighth grade with my brother. No one likes him much. He's in trouble a lot."

"Do you know where he lives?" Lolo asked hopefully.

"No, but I can ask my brother. Richie's brother is in our class, Lolo."

"He is?"

"Yes. Danny Rios. He was in our fifth grade class, too. Remember? He came late in the year."

"Oh, yeah!" said Lolo. "That real quiet kid."

"I know who you mean!" Mario joined in. "He sat in front of me."

"I know 'um, too," said Frankie. "That's it, homes! We just hafta follow Danny home and we got Joker!"

"Then whatcha gonna do?" Mario stormed again. "Knock on the door and ask to see Red-Legs?"

"You could make friends with Danny and ask to play at his house," suggested Lisa.

"Count me out!" Mario grunted. "I'm not goin' near the place."

"Maybe we all shouldn't go, anyway," said Lolo. "You neither, Frankie. Just me!"

"Aah, Lolo! I don't want to miss the fun."

"It's you that Joker's mad at the most. He might not even recognize me." Lolo paused. "I can't do it today, though. I'm supposed 'ta talk with Miss Hernandez after school."

"Do it tomorrow then," urged Frankie, "and I'll back 'ya up . . . from outta sight! I'll be the invisible—"

"Jerk!" interrupted Mario.

Frankie jumped to his feet. "I'll jerk you, *gordito!*"

"C'mon you guys! Quit raggin' on each other! Sit down, Frankie!" Lolo commanded as the bell rang to return to class. "We got the start of a plan!"

"I wish I could help, Lolo," Lisa remarked as they all stood up to leave.

"You've already helped a lot, Lisa!" Lolo assured her. "Thanks!"

♦ ♦ ♦

When the last bell of the day rang, Lolo remained in his seat as the other students headed for the door. "Later, Danny!" he made a point to say to Danny Rios. The boy gave him a surprised look, then smiled weakly and waved as he departed.

As soon as Miss Hernandez finished talking with a few stragglers, Lolo wandered over to her desk.

"What'd you wanna talk to me about, Miss Hernandez?"

"Let's sit down, Lolo," she said, offering him a chair next to her desk. "First, I want you to know how sorry I am about your tarantula. That was a terrible thing that someone did."

"Yeah, I know."

"Do you think there's any chance of getting it back?"

Lolo hesitated, doubtful. "If she's still alive, I might."

"Well," Miss Hernandez sighed, "I'm sorry. Have you thought about choosing something else for your science project?"

Lolo hesitated again, not expecting the question. "No, Miss Hernandez, I haven't."

"Would you like some suggestions?"

"I guess so," Lolo replied, reluctantly.

"Quite a few mammals and reptiles have already been selected," Miss Hernandez noted from a list on her desk. "And several insects. Someone else chose tarantulas, too, and also the black widow spider has been picked. You might want to consider some type of bird or fish, or perhaps a plant. There are a zillion possibilities there."

Lolo's jaw had dropped as if he wanted to say something, but no words came out. He sat slumped in his chair, staring at Miss Hernandez, his brow wrinkled in thought as his mind's voice repeated the words he had just heard. . . . "Someone else chose tarantulas. . . . Someone else chose tarantulas."

"Excuse me, Lolo, but I've got to run to the office for a meeting," said Miss Hernandez, glancing at her watch. "Just give it some thought, and let me know your choice by the end of this week."

Lolo followed her out the door and down the hall to the stairs. He stopped at the top step as the idea struck him. "Danny's got her!" he declared in a hoarse whisper. "That's it! Danny's got Red-Legs!"

14
Strike Out

I'm home! I'm goin' to Frankie's!" Lolo called to Grandfather as he dashed into the house, tossed his books on the living room couch, and raced back outside.

"Okay, *m'ijo*," Grandfather answered from the kitchen, but Lolo was gone.

Frankie lived up and across the street from Lolo's house, and a couple of doors down from Monica's Market. His family's two German shepherds, forever patrolling inside the chain-link fence that surrounded their property, greeted Lolo with friendly yelps and wagging tails. Lolo let himself in through the front gate, paused to pet the shepherds, then shouted, "Frankie! Hey, Frankie!"

In a matter of seconds, Frankie appeared from around the side of the house. "'Ey, Lolo!" he said, wiping perspiration from his forehead with the back of his hand. "I got my bike fixed!"

"Danny Rios has Red-Legs!" Lolo blurted excitedly. "I figured it out!" Then, as an afterthought he added, "I'm glad about your bike."

"'Ey, man. What gives with Danny?"

"Miss Hernandez told me that somebody else is gonna report on tarantulas! So, I figure Joker musta taken Red-Legs, and he gave her to Danny for the science project!"

"Man, ain't that somethin'!" Frankie eyed Lolo with respect. "Now whatcha wanna do?"

"I wanna follow him after school tomorrow, like we talked about. If his mom's there, she might help check him out if he lies to me. . . . You know, look in his room, or somethin'."

"What if she ain't there?"

"Then I'll deal with Danny myself."

The two stood in silence for a moment, then walked over to the front porch steps and sat down. "What about Joker, homes? What if he's there? D'ya want me to get my brothers to back us up?"

Lolo grinned at Frankie. "Not us, Frankie . . . just me . . . and I'll have my bike. I can move fast if there's trouble."

"I'm gonna back 'ya up, man! I'll stay outta sight, but I gotta help some way!"

Lolo shrugged his shoulders. "OK, Frankie. Just don't let Joker see you."

♦ ♦ ♦

"Where's Mario?" Lolo asked when he joined Frankie for lunch the next day.

"I dunno," Frankie replied, his mouth full of pizza. "He must still be mad 'bout yesterday."

"He'll get over it," Lolo said, shaking his head. "He always does."

"Did you tell Lisa what we're gonna do after school?" Frankie asked, curious.

"She's absent today. It's just you and me, Frankie!"

"Yeah!" Frankie sneered, shaking both fists in the air. "And nobody better mess with us!"

♦ ♦ ♦

Lolo waited until Danny Rios reached the door before he left his seat and followed him. Frankie was already in the crowded hallway when Lolo got there, and had started toward the stairs behind Danny. Lolo kept Frankie in sight all the way out to the courtyard. He peeled off from his pursuit to get his bike, then caught up with Frankie in front of the school on Brannick Avenue.

"He's over there!" Frankie pointed toward Hammel Street, then started to run back for his own bike. "Later, homes!"

"Thanks, Frankie." Lolo kept his eyes on Danny until his view was blocked by the corner building. "He's goin' up Hammel toward the pet store!" he shouted.

Frankie waved in acknowledgment.

Lolo raced the short distance to the corner, then slowed when he caught sight of Danny again. Danny was by himself, walking along the sidewalk with his head down.

Lolo stayed half a block behind by riding in figure eights or slowing to the point of barely maintaining balance. He smiled when Danny crossed Hammel at the corner of Hazard Avenue. "Keep goin', punk. Go home," he whispered to himself.

After another block, Danny turned into the neighborhood out of view. Pumping hard, Lolo reached the corner in time to see him enter a yard several houses away. By the time Lolo got there, Danny had disappeared.

The small, wood frame house badly needed repair. Many of its roof shingles had torn away, exposing the attic and weathered support beams. Faded brown paint flaked and curled on its eaves and clapboards. Pieces of cardboard replaced broken panes in its front windows.

Lolo rode his bike across the yard to the slab of cement that served as a porch. He got off long enough to knock on the door, then climbed back on, ready to race out of there if he had to.

The door opened only a crack at first, then swung all the way. A young man, shirtless and barefooted, stood there staring suspiciously at Lolo. Tattoos darkened his muscular arms and chest. A cigarette dangled from his lips. He said nothing, just raised his chin in a reverse nod.

"Can I talk to Danny?" Lolo asked nervously. His right foot rested on the high pedal, ready for a downward push that would send his bike and him back to the street.

"In back," the man snarled, jerking his thumb in the direction of a driveway at the side of the house.

"Thanks," Lolo said with a sigh of relief. He turned his bike and pushed off, coasting to the corner of the house and down the rutted driveway. Ahead of him stood a dilapidated single-car garage, its hinged double doors held closed by an ancient padlock. A house trailer, its once silvery shell now covered with rust, rested its hitch on a double stack of cement blocks alongside the garage.

Lolo stopped at the door of the trailer. Someone lived there according to the laundry hanging from a line stretched from the trailer to the back fence. "Hey, Danny!" Lolo called. "Hey, Danny! C'mon out!"

There was a click, then a thump, as the trailer's door opened outward. Danny Rios stepped to the ground, a half-eaten tortilla in his hand and a surprised look on his face. "What d'ya want?" he asked bluntly.

Lolo sat slumped on the seat of his bike, his angry eyes fixed on the thin face of the smaller boy. "I want my tarantula back!"

"Your tarantula?" Danny's expression changed to puzzlement. "I don't got your tarantula!"

"Yes, you do!" Lolo snapped. "Your brother gave it to you. . . . And he stole it from me!"

"I don't got it!" Danny cried, exasperation mounting in his voice. "I don't know nothin' about it! I never even seen one!"

"HEY, YOU PUNK!" a voice bellowed from the driveway. "WHATCHOO DOIN' HERE?"

Lolo swung his bike around to face the oncoming Joker. "I want my tarantula back!" he yelled, his knuckles turning white from his tight grip on the handlebar.

Joker approached slowly, his cold eyes glaring at Lolo. "It sure ain't around here," he growled.

"Then where is it?" Lolo demanded.

"It's all smashed up like yer gonna be if you don't get outta here!" Joker moved closer, menacingly.

Lolo pushed off, steering his bike around the heavyset teenager.

"And don't hassle *mi hermanito!*" Joker barked angrily, knocking Lolo to the ground with a strong shove. Lolo hit the dirt hard, still straddling the Stingray. Joker stood over him, fists clenched.

"'EY, YOU BIG JOKE!" a hoarse voice called from halfway up the driveway. "WHERE'S YOUR STUPID CAP? I WANNA KNOCK IT OFF AGAIN!"

Joker took one wrathful look at Frankie, and charged after him. "I'M GONNA GET YOU PUNK!" he hollered.

Frankie disappeared up the driveway with Joker in hot pursuit. Lolo untangled his legs from the bike and scrambled to his feet. With no other exit available, he headed up the driveway, too. When he reached the street, he could see Joker at the corner of Hazard, shaking his fists and shouting toward Hammel Street. Lolo swung around and sped off in the other direction.

♦ ♦ ♦

Lolo caught up with Frankie near the pet store. He was parked at the curb, a wide grin spread over his face.

"'Ey, Lolo! That dude's really mad at me now!" He laughed. "But the big Joke can't catch me!"

"Frankie, you're crazy to hassle that guy," Lolo said, catching his breath. "But thanks . . . for savin' my butt."

"*De nada,* homey!" Then in a serious tone, "Whad'ya find out about Red-Legs?"

"I struck out," Lolo replied, his head bowed. "I think she's dead."

Frankie lowered his eyes. "Sorry, Lolo," he said softly.

"Let's split for home, Frankie."

"Yeah, man. Let's split for home."

15
Show Time

"You aren't eating your dinner, *m'ijo*. What's wrong?"

"Nothin', Mom. I'm just not hungry." Lolo sighed, then pushed his chair away from the kitchen table. "Can I go to my room?"

"*¿Está Isidoro enfermo,* Yolanda?" asked Grandfather.

"Are you sick, Lolo?" Lupita was more direct.

"I'm not sick. I just wanna go to my room. Can I?"

"Go ahead, *m'ijo*. I'll check on you in a few minutes."

Lolo stood up. "You don't have to check on me, mom. Nothin's the matter."

Mom waited until she heard the bedroom door close, then gave a sigh herself. "It's that tarantula business. For some reason he really become attached to that spider."

"Why can't Lolo become attached to a regular animal like normal people?" grumbled Lupita, a look of disgust on her face.

"Well, it's his choice. He liked having that kind of a pet. I think I'll go talk with him after we clean up the kitchen."

♦ ♦ ♦

Mom tapped lightly on the door, then opened it a crack and peeked into the room. With lights off and shades down, the dimness made it seem like bedtime. Lolo was lying on his back, eyes closed, arms at his sides. A dozen or so pieces of paper littered the bed beyond the tips of his fingers.

"Those are really nice drawings of your tarantula, *m'ijo*," Mom said softly. "You're becoming quite an artist."

Lolo stirred slightly, then pulled a pillow over his face. "Thanks, Mom," he replied, his voice muffled, "but I don't have a tarantula. Remember?"

"I remember." Mom sat down on the edge of the bed. "Are you going to be all right?"

Lolo adjusted the pillow, but didn't respond.

"You didn't answer me, *m'ijo.* Are you going to be okay?"

"I'll work on it, mom," came the muffled reply. "I just need time to forget Red-Legs."

♦ ♦ ♦

Frankie was waiting outside the front gate when Lolo walked his Stingray around from the backyard. "'Ey, Lolo. We're gonna be late for school. You been gettin' in some extra beauty sleep? Ain't gonna do you no good, man!"

Lolo yawned as he pulled open the gate. "I was awake a lot last night," he said sleepily. "Musta had too much on my mind. Let's go get Mario."

The two friends coasted their bikes down Geraghty a few doors, stopping in front of a well-kept frame house on their right.

"'Ey, MARIO!" Frankie shouted. "LET'S GO, MAN!"

"There's his mom, Frankie."

"He left a few minutes ago!" Mario's mother called from behind the screen door. "He thought you went without him!"

Both boys waved to her as they pushed off down the street.

"Try to keep up with me, homes!"

"I'll be there waitin' for you, Frankie!"

◆ ◆ ◆

"There's the bell!" Lolo called out as the two swung their bikes onto Brannick Avenue.

"I heard it, homes. Let's jump the curb and cut across the grass."

By the time they parked at the bicycle racks,

most of the students had lined up in the courtyard. Frankie could see his classmates and Mr. Baca standing in their usual place near the building entrance. "Meetcha at recess, Lolo," he said as he headed in their direction.

"Later, Frankie." Lolo started off toward the flag-pole where his class always gathered. He reached the end of the boys' line just as the flag salute began. Directly in front of him stood Danny Rios.

"What's up, Danny?" Lolo spoke quietly when the salute was over. Danny turned quickly, then stepped back, raising his fists.

He looked up at Lolo with fear in his eyes.

"Whatcha . . . whatcha gonna do?" he stammered.

"Relax, man. I'm not gonna bother you. The line's movin'. Let's get goin'."

They both walked fast to catch up with their classmates. Danny kept as much distance as he could between himself and Lolo, frequently looking nervously over his shoulder.

Lolo was disappointed that Lisa hadn't returned to school. It was as if he had no one to talk to, even though he had many friends among his classmates. When he reached his seat, he slumped into it wishing he could go back home.

Math period dragged by until a pop quiz was passed out, then the clock hands seemed to be in a race with each other. When the quiz was over, Miss Hernandez brought up another subject.

"I want you to begin your science research today!" Several students clapped their hands eagerly. Miss Hernandez smiled, then continued, "Yes, we've got exciting topics to learn about, and lots of work to do. I've stocked our classroom library with a wide variety of reference books. You have the instructions I gave you yesterday for note taking and outlining. There are art materials for you on the table near my desk when you're ready to prepare illustrations, posters, or dioramas. You should each be ready to get off to a great start. Raise your hands as questions come up and I'll be around to see you."

Lolo slouched in his seat watching all the activity unfold around him. Everyone seemed to know what to do. Everyone seemed to have an interesting science project to work on . . . except him.

"How are you doing, Lolo?" he heard his teacher's voice from behind him.

He turned in his seat. "Not so good, Miss Hernandez."

"What topic did you finally choose for your project?

Lolo shrugged his shoulders. "I don't have a topic."

A slight frown came over Miss Hernandez's face. "Well, Lolo, I thought that might be the case. I'll tell you what! Only two students have chosen birds for a topic. One picked eagles, the other chose hawks. There's a well-illustrated book about birds on my desk. Go get it and look it over. There are lots of possibilities you can consider." She started to move on down the aisle. "I want you to get started today."

Now Lolo's face had the frown. He remained in his seat for another minute, then slowly got up and strolled over to his teacher's desk. "Birds!" he growled under his breath. "Dumb birds!"

♦ ♦ ♦

Lolo hurried to the bicycle racks after the last bell. He had his bike unchained and ready to mount by the time Frankie and Mario arrived.

"You goin' to a fire, homey?" Frankie asked jokingly.

"Let's just go," said Lolo, irritated.

"What do you guys wanna do after we get home?" Mario asked as he pulled his BMX out of the rack. "Do you wanna ride bikes some more?"

"How 'bout we go to the park and shoot baskets?" Frankie suggested. "Whatcha think Lolo?"

"I think I'll think about it," Lolo replied, still irritated.

The three pedaled slowly along Brannick, weaving to avoid students on foot, and calling out to friends. They crossed to the far side of Hammel and headed up the busy street with Mario taking the lead. They rode in silence until they approached Animales Domésticos.

"Hey, there's Mr. Verdugo!" Mario shouted, pointing ahead and across the street. "That must be his van!"

Mr. Verdugo had just gotten out of a Dodge van parked in front of his shop. He walked to the back of the van and opened its rear doors.

"It looks like he's gonna unload somethin'!" Mario informed the others.

"Let's give'um a hand, homeys!" Frankie swerved his bike to cross the street.

"Hey, let's not go over there!" Lolo cried as Mario started across, too. "I don't wanna do this," he muttered to himself as he reluctantly followed his two friends.

"Can we help you, Mr. Verdugo?" Frankie asked first.

"Yeah, can we help?" echoed Mario.

"Hi, boys! Sure! I'm taking my tarantulas to the fair this afternoon. It's time for them to put on their show for my sister's customers. You can help me put their tarantulariums in the van. I'll be right back with the first one."

Lolo stayed on his bike as Frankie and Mario dismounted and crawled inside the van.

"You can hand it to us," Mario said as Mr. Verdugo returned with his load. Lolo recognized the Texas cinnamon.

"This one isn't as big as Red-Legs," observed Mario. "It's color is lighter, too."

Mr. Verdugo set the tarantularium in the back of the Dodge. "You can use those straps to secure it while I go get the next one," he directed.

He was back in a minute with another glass box.

"Geez!" Mario jumped out of the van. "I don't wanna get close to that one!"

Lolo knew it was the Honduran black velvet without even looking.

"Here, Frankie. Strap this one down. One more to go!" said Mr. Verdugo as he went back in the shop.

"Ey, Mario! Get yer butt in here! This big, black dude wants to show you its fangs!"

"No way! I'm stayin' out here!"

Lolo started to laugh, then remembered that none of this was fun to him.

"Here comes the last one," Mr. Verdugo announced, setting the third tarantularium down next to Frankie. Then he turned and nodded to Lolo, "I know we all wish that Red-Legs was here to go along."

Lolo nodded in response, but didn't speak.

"I'll finish it, Frankie. It's time to close the

shop and take off. *¡Gracias amigos!*"

"*De nada,* Mr. Verdugo," said Frankie, climbing out of the van.

"Yea, you're welcome, Mr. Verdugo," said Mario, mounting his bike.

"Bye," said Lolo, pushing off towards home.

16

Good Grip!

"Lolo! Frankie and Mario are at the front door!" Lupita hollered from the kitchen. It was Saturday morning and Lolo was helping Grandfather pick peaches in the back yard.

"I'm coming!" Lolo hollered back. "*Abuelo,* can I go now?"

"*Sí, m'ijo. Tenemos bastantes.*"

When Lolo got to the open front door, he saw a large cardboard box—taller than his friends—standing on the porch next to Frankie. Mario stood nearby with his arms loaded with pieces of plywood.

"What's up?" said Lolo.

"Where you been, homey?" Frankie asked cheerfully. "We didn't see you yesterday!"

"Did you ditch school?" Mario teased, a grin on his face.

"That's real funny, Mario. I wasn't feeling good.

I musta caught somethin'."

"You look okay now, homes! Can you play?"

"What're you guys gonna do?" Lolo asked.

"We're gonna fix up the fort, man!" Frankie said brightly. "C'mon with us!"

"Yeah, c'mon, Lolo!" Mario chimed in. "We need you to hold up the new roof!"

Lolo hesitated, then shook his head. "I don't—"

"C'mon, homey!" Frankie interrupted. "Forget about *arañas,* man! We just wanna play in our fort!"

Lolo hesitated again.

"C'mon, Lolo!" Mario pleaded. "Frankie wore himself out carryin' that box over here. He'll have a heart attack if you don't help him the rest of the way!"

Lolo stepped out onto the porch, glared at the huge box, then growled, "Let's do it."

They carried the box around to the backyard, lifted it over the fence, and slid it down the hill to the remains of Fort Araña.

"Did you bring somethin' that'll cut cardboard?" Lolo asked.

"Got my blade right here!" Frankie assured him, patting the front pocket of his ragged jeans.

"Get it out then, and let's get this done," Lolo said impatiently, standing the box up on one end. "I'll hold it and you cut."

"I'm gonna work on the wall while you guys do

that," said Mario, dropping his load of plywood on the ground. He started toward the front of the fort, then stopped abruptly and turned to his two friends. "Hey, look who's comin' up the hill!" he whispered anxiously.

"It's Rogelio . . . all by himself," said Lolo, warily.

Frankie didn't say anything. His staring brown eyes locked on to the lanky fourteen-year-old advancing slowly up the hillside. When Rogelio passed the battered piece of cardboard that was once the fort's roof, Frankie bent down to pick up several large dirt clods. Lolo and Mario armed themselves the same way.

"Hey! I'm not gonna do nothin' to you," Rogelio called to them. "I just wanna give you dudes some free advice."

"We don't need no advice from you, man," snarled Frankie, as he tossed a clod into the air a few inches and caught it, then tossed and caught it again.

Rogelio came a little closer, then stopped. "You'd better listen anyway homeboy. Don't mess with Joker—that dudes got somthin' wrong in his head. He'll hurt you, man."

Lolo stepped forward, "What about my tarantula?" he asked angrily.

"Yea, too bad about that. We got inside the fort

and Joker stood up fast when he saw the spider. That's how the roof got busted up. I think he's scared of spiders—big ones anyway."

"You knocked down the wall, too!" said Mario accusingly.

"We were just messin'," Rogelio tried to explain. "I told Joker that I was gonna let the spider loose on him. He pushed me, and I fell backwards into the wall. That's when the jar flew out of my hands."

"What happened to my tarantula!" Lolo exploded, smashing a clod near Rogelio's feet.

"Take it easy, man!" said Rogelio, backing away. "When the jar broke, the spider ran into a hole!"

"Which hole!" Lolo shouted.

Rogelio pointed at the remains of the jar. "I think it was that one near the glass."

Lolo rushed over to the breakage and spotted a hole a few inches from it. Falling to his knees, he peered into its darkness. "I see webbing!" he called out. Then, jumping to his feet, he took off up the slope toward his house.

"Where're ya goin', homes?" Frankie yelled.

Lolo just kept on running.

◆ ◆ ◆

"Mom!" Lolo shouted as he burst in through the back door. "I need some meat!"

"What on earth for?" Mom asked in surprise.

"Mom, please hurry! I'm gonna catch Red-Legs!"

"There's ground beef for the tacos we're having for dinner, but you can only have a little bit!"

"I don't need much, Mom!" Lolo helped himself from the package Mom took from the refrigerator. "*Abuelo!* Can I have some string?" he asked Grandfather who had come into the kitchen in response to the commotion.

"*Sí, en el cajón.*" Grandfather pointed to the drawer behind Lolo.

Lolo wrapped the small amount of meat in a paper napkin, found the string, then raced back out the door.

♦ ♦ ♦

"Here he comes!" announced Mario as Lolo came running down the hillside. "He sure is in a hurry!"

Lolo slowed to a walk as he approached the fort, pausing briefly to pick up a flat piece of shale about the size of a quarter. The others gathered around curiously as he took a pinch of meat from the napkin, pressed it on top of the rock, and tied on the string. They hardly noticed Lolo's mother and grandfather coming down the hill to join them.

"Don't anybody move or make a noise," Lolo commanded as he walked over to the broken jar. He crouched down on one knee and held the string in a ready position. As the others craned their necks to see better, he lowered the baited rock closer to the hole. It came to rest about an inch or so from the dark, round opening. Everyone waited, hardly breathing, for some reaction to the bait.

It happened so quickly. Out from the hole came the tarantula, pouncing on the meat with its front legs and chelicerae. Lolo reacted almost as fast. He pulled the spider away from the hole, then reached down and gripped it between his thumb and forefinger. He lifted it straight up and held it away from his body. "I've got her!" he declared, grinning broadly at the others. "I've got Red-Legs!"

"Geez! It's gonna bite you!" Mario cried. He shuddered and backed away.

Frankie's face split into a wide grin. "Oh, man!" he whooped. "Oh, man! You found the *araña*, homey!"

Rogelio stepped closer, staring at the suspended Red-Legs. "How can you touch it, man? That thing's ugly!"

Grandfather walked over to Lolo. "Here, *m'ijo*. Put your *tarántula* in this." He held out an empty coffee can that he had brought with him.

From a few yards away, Mom called to Lolo, "If you find a lid for that can, I'll drive you down to the pet store, *m'ijo!*"

♦ ♦ ♦

The fourth tarantularium was still on top of the display case when Lolo, Mom, Frankie, and Mario entered Animales Domésticos. Mr. Verdugo excused himself from a customer and came right over to them.

"I found Red-Legs!" Lolo sang out, holding up the coffee can.

"Terrific news!" Mr. Verdugo cheered, clapping his hands. He took the can from Lolo and removed the plastic lid. "Where was she?" he asked, taking a closer look.

"She was in a hole near the broken jar." Lolo explained. "I got her out like my *abuelo* showed me."

"He picked it up with his bare hand!" Mario spoke up, admiringly.

"Good for you, Lolo!" said Mr. Verdugo.

"Can we still go to the fair?" Frankie asked, eagerly.

"You bet we can! How about you, Yolanda? Would you like to join us? There's plenty of room in my van."

"Why . . . I guess I could," Mom responded, blushing slightly. "It sounds like fun!"

"Great! I'll pick you all up at eight o'clock. Red-Legs can get acquainted with her new tarantularium right now. I'll have her packed in the van and ready to go when I see you."

"We're goin' to the fair!" Lolo shouted.

"We're goin' to the fair!" everyone joined in. "Goin' to the fair!"

17
Goin' to the Fair!

Sunday morning traffic was heavy, but fast. The Dodge van roared along at fifty-five miles per hour, with Lolo, Frankie, and Mario buckled snugly in the seat behind Mr. Verdugo and Mom, and the tarantularium secured by straps in the back.

"Are all these cars goin' to the fair?" Lolo asked.

"No, I don't think so," Mr. Verdugo laughed, "but there will be lots of people there!"

"I don't drive freeways myself," said Mom, "so all of this is new to Lolo and me."

"I don't have to drive them often," Mr. Verdugo replied, "but for a trip like this, it's the fastest way to go."

"Are we almost there?" asked Mario.

"Just about another mile to our exit, then about ten minutes to the fairgrounds."

When they turned off the freeway, they drove

by hills with grass and trees on them instead of streets and houses.

"Look at the horses!" said Mario, pointing to his left.

"Man, I ain't never seen one up close," Frankie remarked.

"You will today!" said Mr. Verdugo. "Lots of them!"

After a few more minutes, Mr. Verdugo stopped the van behind a long line of slow-moving cars. "We're almost there," he said. "We just need to get parked."

Lolo had never seen as many cars in one place as there were in the parking lot they entered. "There's a million cars here!" he said, wide-eyed, as he unbuckled his seat belt and sat up straight to get a better view. Mr. Verdugo followed the directions of waving parking-lot attendants, and soon pulled into an empty space. When Lolo got out, he felt surrounded by an ocean of automobiles.

"Let's take a tram so I won't have to carry the tarantularium so far," suggested Mr. Verdugo, closing the back door of the van.

"Is that a tram?" Lolo asked, pointing at a long, open, bus-like vehicle heading their way.

"That's it! Be ready to get on when it stops. It'll give us a free ride to the ticket booths."

◆ ◆ ◆

"Look at the rides we can go on!" Lolo called to the others after entering the fairgrounds. "Even a Ferris wheel!"

"I smell popcorn!" said Mario. "And they got cotton candy, too!"

"We can shoot guns at things over there!" said Frankie, pointing to a row of game booths from which the popping of air rifles could be heard.

Lolo turned to Mr. Verdugo, awed by all the exciting things he saw. "There's so much!" he said. "Where do we start?"

"This is only a small part of it. There's lots more! Mexican Village is over to the left. Let's go over there first." He nodded toward a cluster of canopies and tile-roofed buildings surrounded by a white adobe wall. "That's where my sister has her *tiendita*. She sells jewelry, mostly. Red-Legs is going to help her."

◆ ◆ ◆

Red-Legs turned out to be the most popular of the four tarantulas whose glass homes nestled among displays of colorful bracelets, earrings, and necklaces. "How much do you want for it?" some people asked. One man offered fifty dollars for Red-Legs and the tarantularium. When Lolo heard about that, he shook his head. "No way! I'm not sellin'!"

◆ ◆ ◆

It was almost nine o'clock when they said good night to the tarantulas and walked back to the van. "You're finally slowing down!" said Mr. Verdugo, pausing to let the boys catch up with him and Mom. The three were yawning, hardly able to keep their eyes open.

"We're tired, Mr. Verdugo," said Lolo, "but we saw everything!"

"I musta seen every kinda farm animal there is," claimed Frankie, his voice a sleepy drawl. "But, man! Those horses are somethin' else. I'm gonna have me a big, black stallion some day and a ranch where it can live."

"Did you guys see those giant rabbits?" Mario asked. "The sign said they weigh more than twenty pounds. I could raise rabbits in my backyard. I'm gonna ask my mom."

"I liked watchin' that lady draw people with colored chalk," Lolo joined in. "She's real good. Maybe I can draw like that if I keep practicin'."

"Yolanda," Mr. Verdugo said, turning to Mom, "what did you enjoy the most today?"

"The cute little shops in Mexican Village, and the beautiful earrings you bought for me. And sitting in the shade watching the *folklorico* and eating those delicious enchiladas from Rose's food stand. And going to the horse races. And so much more. Thank you, Alex."

"Yea, thanks Mr. Verdugo!" each of the boys chimed in.

"You are all very welcome. By the way, there are pillows in the back of the van. You boys can sleep on the way home."

"That's a good idea, Lolo," said Mom. "You have school tomorrow."

"No problem, Mom! I'm gonna like school better now that I've got Red-Legs back. I gotta tell Miss Hernandez that my science project is gonna be about tarantulas after all." Then, remembering, he said under his breath, "Me and some other guy."

"Science project? Liking school? Is that you talking, Lolo, or am I dreaming?"

"It's really me, Mom. Would you like to touch the hand that picks up tarantulas?"

"That's funny, Lolo . . . real funny . . . about as funny as brain tacos. Remind me—"

Lolo interrupted, "I know, I know, Mom. I'll remind you to laugh when we get home."

18

Partners

"L isa!" Lolo called as he approached the double line of students forming behind Miss Hernandez.

"Hi, Lolo!" Lisa looked excited, leaving her place to greet him. "I'm glad to see you! I feel like I've been gone forever!"

"You're just now comin' back?" Lolo asked.

"I had the flu. It was awful, but I'm finally over it. What did I miss?"

"I stayed home Thursday and Friday, so I don't know what we missed around here, but I got Red-Legs back!"

"You did!" Lisa squealed, grabbing Lolo's arm. "Oh, I'm so happy! I want to hear all about it! Was it that boy you asked me about? Did he have Red-Legs?"

"No, Joker didn't have her. I thought Danny Rios had her, but he didn't either. I found her in a hole near the fort."

"Oh, Lolo!" Lisa sighed. "That's the best news! Now maybe you and I can study about tarantulas together after all!" She looked at him hopefully.

"Sure! That'll be okay," Lolo consented. "I'll let you hold Red-Legs, too, if that's still somethin' you wanna do."

Lisa smiled, her eyes sparkling. "And I'll let you hold Blondie if you want to."

Lolo gave her a questioning look. "Who's Blondie?"

"Blondie's my tarantula!" Lisa replied, laughing. "Her color is really a light beige, but she's called a Mexican blond. She's smaller than Red-Legs and she doesn't mind being held."

Lolo stared at Lisa in amazement. "You? You have a tarantula?"

"Yes! I'm not kidding!" Lisa smiled understandingly. "I didn't want to say anything about her after you lost Red-Legs. She belonged to my dad until I talked him into giving her to me. That was at the beginning of the summer."

Lolo shook his head, then let a grin spread across his face. "I guess we really are partners!" A loud squeak from the public address system interrupted him. Miss Hernandez looked at Lolo and held a finger up to her lips. Lolo nodded at her and whispered to Lisa, "Let's get in line. We can talk some more when we get to class."

◆ ◆ ◆

"Miss Hernandez! I got my tarantula back!" Lolo announced cheerfully as his teacher greeted him at the classroom door.

"That's wonderful, Lolo!" she replied. "Why don't you share that with the class this morning? They'll be glad to hear the good news!"

Lolo paused, looking unsure of himself. He never had liked speaking in front of his class about anything.

"Okay!" he said firmly, his doubts passing quickly.

Sitting down at his desk, he turned around to face Lisa. "I'm gonna share about Red-Legs . . . and about the fair, too . . . and about my mom changin' her mind and lettin' me keep Red-Legs in the back yard. And I'll tell about us bein' science partners, if that's okay with you."

It was.

Glossary

Adiós—Goodbye

Abuelo—Grandfather

Amigos—Friends

Araña—Spider

Bueno—Good

Chicas—Girls

Cholos—*(slang)* Punks; dudes

Compadres—Friends

De nada—Literally, It is nothing, meaning "You're Welcome."

Folklorico—Traditional dancing

Gracias—Thank you

Gordito—*(slang)* Fatty; literally, little fat one

Hola—Hello

Homes, *or* **Homey**—Short for Homeboy, a friend from your neighborhood

Maestra—Teacher

M'ijo—A contraction of Mi Hijo, literally, My Son or My Child. A term of endearment, also used by non relatives.

No problema—No problem

Sí—Yes

Suavecito—*(slang)* Take it easy

Tarántula—Tarantula

Tía—Aunt

Tiendita—Little store; booth

Translations

p. 9   **Ven m'ijo.**—Come in, my son.
       No son peligrosas.—They aren't dangerous.

p. 10 **Pues, vamos a ver.**—Well, we'll see.
       ¿Que vas a hacer con una tarántula?—What are you going to do with a tarantula?
       Vamos a necesitar algo para guardarla.—We are going to need something to keep it in.

p. 11 **En qué piensas?**—What are you thinking about?

p. 12 **¡Ay, los muchachos!**—Ahh, boys! *(said with exasperation)*

p. 13 **No,...pero lo ha visto como se hace.**—No, but I've seen it done before.
En México, es regular.—In Mexico, it's common.
Necesito una piedrita como el tamaño de una moneda.—I need a little rock that's about the size of a coin.

p. 14 **¿Estás listo?**—Are you ready?

p. 15 **Ahora cuidala bien.**—Now take good care of it.

p. 17 **Animales Domésticos**—Domestic Animals, pets

p. 24 **¡Quítala de aquí! ¡Pronto!**—Get it out of here! Quick!
Calmate, m'ija, no son peligrosas—Calm down, daughter, they aren't dangerous.

p. 25 **Lo qué tu digas...No hay problema**—Whatever you say....There's not a problem.

p. 32 **¡Ganamos! ¡Somos los mejores!**—We win! We're the best!

p. 34 **¡Vamos al parque!**—Let's go to the park!

p. 37 **loca en la cabeza**—crazy in the head

p. 44 **No sé.**—I don't know.
Tal vez es mejor si tú hablas con el Señor Verdugo.
—Perhaps it's better if you talk with Mr. Verdugo.

p. 59 **De dónde vienes?**—Where did you come from?
Pero hay duraznos frescos—But there are fresh peaches.
Está bien.—That's fine.

p. 83 **Mi hermanito**—my little brother

p. 86 **¿Está Isidoro enfermo?**—Is Isidore sick?

p. 95 **Tenemos bastantes.**—We have enough.

p. 99 **Si, en el cajón.**—Yes, in the drawer.

About the Author

KIRK REEVE began writing short stories about children during his years as an elementary school principal in Los Angeles. *Lolo and Red-Legs*, Kirk's first novel, is based on a lengthy, emotion-filled conversation he had with a young man who described his boyhood years growing up on Geraghty Avenue in Las Lomitas. The young man's experiences were the foundation for Lolo's. Mr. Reeve divides his time between writing, teaching, and operating a home business in Orange County, California.